# Labyrinth

Also by Burhan Sönmez

*Istanbul Istanbul*
*Sins and Innocents*

# BURHAN SÖNMEZ

*Translated from the Turkish by Ümit Hussein*

# Labyrinth

OTHER PRESS

NEW YORK

*Production editor: Yvonne E. Cárdenas*
*Text designer: Jennifer Daddio / Bookmark Design & Media Inc.*
*This book was set in Adobe Garamond and Hypatia by*
*Alpha Design & Composition of Pittsfield, NH*

10 9 8 7 6 5 4 3 2 1

Library of Congress Cataloging-in-Publication Data

Names: Sönmez, Burhan, author. | Hussein, Ümit, translator.
Title: Labyrinth / Burhan Sönmez ; translated from the Turkish by Ümit Hussein.
Other titles: Labirent. English
Description: New York : Other Press, [2019]
Identifiers: LCCN 2019015339 | ISBN 9781590510988 (pbk.) |
    ISBN 9781590511008 (ebook)
Classification: LCC PL248.S565 L3313 2019 | DDC 894/.3534—dc23
    LC record available at https://lccn.loc.gov/2019015339

*Publisher's Note*: This is a work of fiction. Names, characters, places, and incidents either are the product of the author's imagination or are used fictitiously, and any resemblance to actual persons, living or dead, events, or locales is entirely coincidental.

*It only takes two facing mirrors*
*to construct a labyrinth.*

J. L. BORGES, *SEVEN NIGHTS*

*It is not man who discovers the word,*
*it is the word that comes to him.*

PASTOR EDOUARD DE MONTMOLLIN'S SERMON AT BORGES'S FUNERAL

# A Leap Off the Bosphorus Bridge

# 1

An alarm clock goes off. It sounds like the bell summoning the weary crew members of a cargo ship to dinner. But who remembers cargo ships? It's coming from the next apartment, or perhaps from a dream. From the dream of someone sleeping in the next apartment. A breeze blows in through the open balcony door. The net curtain billows. Whatever season this may be, the cool of the morning gives it a certain freshness. As the bottom of the net curtain flutters towards the bed, the sound of the alarm clock grows louder. Without opening his eyes, Boratin reaches out and tries to turn it off. His hand gropes the bedside table. He stops. He pauses for a moment, then tries again. When he fails to locate the clock, he opens his eyes. Outside, the day is dawning. The objects in the room are hazy, silhouetted. Where is he? It doesn't look like a hospital room. The blanket, the balcony, and the window are different. No, this isn't a hospital. I think I've come home. The sky is visible from the window. There are medicine bottles at the far end of the bedside table. Although the medicine helps him sleep, it doesn't soothe his headache. His eyes close again. His hand falls onto the pillow. As the leaves of a tree rustle somewhere close to the balcony, the coolness caresses his bare arms.

Boratin awakes when the sky is bright and the wind has abated. The net curtain is still. Outside there is a murmur that has gradually built up and intensified since it first started out in distant neighborhoods. He looks around him, trying to ascertain whether he has ever woken up here before. The room is spacious. The walls are a plain ivory color, but the maple veneer of the wardrobe opposite him is too light. A darker shade would have looked better. Who chose that wardrobe, was it me? Boratin questions his own taste. When they brought him here last night he had hoped that this unfamiliar house might trigger some memories in the light of day. The balcony door, the wardrobe, and the bedside table remind him of a hotel room where he is staying for the first time. The only familiar objects are the medicine bottles. He perches on the edge of the bed. He winces at the pain in his chest. He pulls up his undershirt and inspects his ribs. He walks over to the mirror to get a better view. One of his right ribs is broken. He touches it. He feels the burning under his skin. He was lucky, that's what they said. Only one fracture. His body had suffered no other injuries: Memory loss doesn't count as a bodily injury. He raises his eyes and looks at his face. The face he met a week ago. It's that new. Hello stranger, he says. He can tell from its lip movements that the face in the mirror is answering him with the same words. Just like last night. When he came home yesterday everything was silent. He wandered through the rooms with careful footsteps, as though exploring a museum, gingerly picking his way around the ornaments and guitars. He took his medication out of the hospital bag. He drank two glasses of water. He examined his face in the mirror. He removed his shirt, trousers, and socks. He lay down, closed his eyes, and waited without moving. He counted his inhalations and exhalations. He hadn't forgotten how to count. Forty-one, forty-two, forty-three. Then he drifted off.

At the hospital they had told him to stay calm. You've lost your memory, don't be afraid, you'll get it back eventually, they had said. First they had dealt with his rib, then they had wanted to know what could have happened to this man who was trying hard to create a whole person out of his broken rib and his blank memory. It's strange, he had said to his doctor, you're more interested in me than I am. It's my job, the doctor had replied. Losing your memory may seem very daunting Boratin Bey, but your situation isn't that bad, considering. At least we know who you are and where you live, thanks to the cards in your wallet. You may not remember, but those details are part of who you are, just like that tattoo on your back that you don't know where or why you had done. For now you own things that you can't explain, things that will take shape over time. Whatever your past story may be, perhaps what you wanted was to get away from some aspect of this world. You were bold enough to attempt it, and you even succeeded. You fulfilled your objective in a way you could never have imagined. By taking a leap off the Bosphorus Bridge.... From now on you'll map out a much better path. Tell me Doctor, do you dispense this much hope to all your patients along with their medication? If so I'll tell you this: My mind, which hasn't got a single word about myself in it, is bursting with facts about other things. The names of ancient philosophers, the colors of soccer teams, the words of the first astronaut who went to the moon. I can't find any clues leading to myself in my cache, I can't even remember my name. You told me that was my name, and I accepted it.

I search for a comforting sign in my reflection, an expression that will point me in the right direction. I place my ear on the face in the mirror, where its mouth was. It's smooth. Cool. I hear the roar of a wave that got trapped here many eras ago. Dark desires. The dank odor of a cellar. I'm approaching the time I used to live in but have tumbled out of. I am about to try descending into my memory down a different ladder and lighting the blue lantern in the vault of the past, when I am startled by the sound of ringing. Is it coming from inside or outside? It sounds like the alarm on the clock that rang all night. I follow the sound out into the hallway. I walk past a gloomy painting. I spy a black and red telephone at the opposite end of the lounge. I stop and wonder what to do. The telephone falls silent before I can make up my mind. It has an old-fashioned receiver, with keys that you don't press but dial. It sits in a holder made of decorative wrought gold metal, the kind that old people like.

The telephone starts ringing again. This time with more determination. If I answer, an unfamiliar voice will ask me how I am. It won't feel the need to introduce itself. It will simply assume I know it. When I remain silent it will repeat its question. After a moment's hesitation it will start speaking for me. It will talk about things we have to do. It will remind me of some get-together or meal we're supposed to be attending. It will prattle on about life's misfortunes. After a brief show of compassion it will start to reproach me in an aggrieved tone. It will enumerate every evil in existence, naming someone who has fallen victim to each one, and then, without giving me a chance to hang up, heap the blame for the victims' doom on my head. Because I do not speak, it will jump from topic to topic. When the subject moves on to the good turns I have done it, the voice will soften, it will say it is thanks to me that it has been able to enjoy life's blessings, but that it doesn't understand how I ended up this way. I will seize the opportunity to intervene. I will say that I don't understand how I ended up this way either. I will ask it to help me, and if it knows any secrets about me, to let me in on them right away. As I have lost my memory, I have lost the life I have led all these years too, I'm back at zero. I will plead with it for mercy, as though it were a guardian holding my past in the palm of its hand. I will select the most beseeching words. I will tell the voice on the other end of the telephone a story that has stuck in a corner of my mind. The future is as unattainable as the past. I can't use the stars to guide me. I can feel an avalanche approaching fast, mingling into the sounds of traffic, plunging and tumbling behind towers and sky-scrapers. My heart is telling me I have to hurry. I rush to draw the curtains. I pull the curtains tightly so no light will seep in through any crack. The telephone falls silent.

## 2

I am sitting on the sofa in the lounge, waiting for the telephone to start ringing again. I notice a figurine on the mantelpiece, between a row of candles of all different colors. I recognize the mother and son in the marble figurine. Mary is holding Jesus in her arms and gazing at his lifeless face. The curve of the marble flows from Mary's forehead to her nose, and from there to her lips, like water. Jesus' chest is bare, you can count every one of his right ribs. Mary clutches her son with one hand and raises the other into the air, as though pleading for help. Although I recognize them, I can't place them in time. How many years has it been? Has it been just a few years since their suffering, or a few thousand?

While outside it's bustling with street sellers, rowdy children, and taxi drivers listening to loud Arabesk music, despite everything, I feel safe in this house that, for some unfathomable reason, is mine. People should familiarize themselves with objects before familiarizing themselves with other people, and carve out their place among them. The rest is a matter of asking questions, listening to sounds, wandering through rooms, and waiting for answers. I don't know how long I'll have to wait. What if I never get an answer? There are logs piled up beside the fireplace. A wooden cabinet is filled with bottles of drink. The lounge is occupied by guitars, records, coffee tables, chandeliers, rugs, a table and chairs, all looking as though they have never once shifted from their places. The crystals on the chandelier above my head hang down in multitudes, growing in number until they have taken over the entire ceiling—you can't get a view of one side of the chandelier from the other. Even prolific families of snakes could nest in the multiple rows of crystals and live out their lives there. At midnight when the entire city is sleeping (does the city sleep?) the snakes slither from the chandelier and spread out over the ceiling, wandering over the walls with their immortal fluid, hissing as they glide behind the curtains, curling and winding and exchanging venom as they copulate; then, at the first light of day, their blood appeased and their skin glistening, they return to their nests. If every house has its secret proprietors, the proprietors of this one are the snakes, they are the source of both curses and good fortune.

I wonder if I have ever been caught up in this bizarre daydream before. As I gaze at each individual piece of furniture, looking for a compass to guide me, I realize that everything in this house is elderly. The table and chairs are the same age as extinct trees, the rugs the same age as nomad tents. I might not be able to differentiate between one year and a thousand years, but I do know that this life belongs to death. And I also realize that it's not what I know that I should be suspicious of, but what I don't know. I ask myself why, when the noises in the street have their own meaning, this house doesn't offer me any meaning. Within the mute walls, I wonder which of us has become forgetful, have I forgotten my house, or has my house forgotten me? Which of us has been giving nothing away since yesterday; who, like a blind beggar, has been suspended in a void and become withdrawn? I wonder what my connection is to the three guitars on metal stands in front of me. Next to the guitars is a record player and a record rack. There are a few old album covers hanging on the back wall. The first album on the top row is Delta Blues. Next to it are Bessie Smith, Howlin' Wolf, and Chicago Blues albums. The album cover on the bottom row says "Submarine." The whitewash of the wall behind the inexplicably solitary Submarine sparkles. When I realize that the shine is coming from the sunlight, I turn and look. The curtain is open a tiny crack. The light enters and shines through it. I get up and pull the curtains open. I am dazzled by the light that floods in. I take a few tentative steps towards the center of the lounge.

I feel as though my life in this house is nothing but a series of repetitions. I lose my memory over and over again: Each time I open my eyes in the hospital and after a few days I come home. I wake up with the same headache. I learn how to divide time into minutes and hours. The names of seasons are pleasing to me, in any language. I go to sleep late and when, one morning, I wake up in the hospital again, having lost my memory, I realize I am caught up in the world's eternal cycle. Empty. Alone. I think that these thoughts that assail me at home too, now that I have left the hospital, are driving me to the brink of madness. I search for meaning in objects by asking questions. The velvet sofa cover is beautiful. The red of the velvet is beautiful. The Mary in the figurine is beautiful. But what does *beautiful* mean? If I hadn't lost my memory, would I know?

I caress the furry velvet on the sofa. I observe my joints while moving my fingers as though they were part of a machine. A machine with human feelings. It has a brain, but from time to time the program inside it rewinds to the beginning. It comes and goes between zero and one. The world too consists of the movement between those two numbers. Sometimes that movement, which is also known as time, comes to life at my fingertips, like a newborn animal. An animal and a machine have come together in the same body, the animal searches for clues in the sleekness of the fabric and the chandelier crystals. It receives vague questions in reply. That's why my rib hurts. Placing my hand over my rib, I walk to the kitchen at the end of the hallway. As I am about to step into the same kitchen I went into last night, I stop and try to recall the positions of the sink and the fridge. Once I feel certain I turn my head and look inside. I relax when I see them both in the right place. The kitchen in my memory and the actual kitchen are the same. Life can be that simple. As long as my mind doesn't play games with the world, or the world with my mind. I stride into the kitchen confidently. I pick up the jug of water from the table and fill a glass. I listen to the sound of the water pouring from the jug. I raise the glass to the window and examine it in the light. As I drink the water I wonder whether light has a taste. I wipe the drops of water lingering on my lips with my fingers. At that point I am not aware that the glass I have placed on the edge of the table is falling. Startled by the sound of the glass crashing to the ground and smashing, I retreat two paces. I lean against the fridge. I lock my fingers together. I look at the shards scattered between the cupboards and in the doorway. I feel as if the world I have been trying to piece together for the past few days has shattered like glass and is once again lying around me in pieces. Just as I am about to grab the counter beside me for support, I jump, this time at the sound of an ear-piercing bell. I am being assailed from all sides. The sound of the bell isn't like the telephone's vibrating ring. And it isn't an insistent alarm clock ringing in the next apartment either. It's ringing very near me, inside my head.

## 3

Open the door Boratin, it's me, Bek. Struggling to match the voice outside with the face forming in my mind, I reach for the lock. I turn the key slowly, in an attempt to buy time for my memory. I open the door a crack, as though it's liable to open out into empty space. I look at the man waiting in the dimly lit hallway. I know his face, he's my friend (is he my friend?) who came to visit me in the hospital twice. He was worried on his first visit, reassured on the second. His voice inspired trust. Are you well? Yes. I went to the hospital this morning, they said you'd been discharged, I thought you were staying till the beginning of next week? I don't know, I told them yesterday I wanted to be discharged and they said okay. How could they let you leave when there's no one to take care of you? They didn't let me leave straightaway, they phoned you, only your phone was switched off. But I didn't want to spend another moment in that crowded ward listening to all those sick people groaning.

We go into the lounge and sit down; I sit on the sofa where I was before, he sits on the armchair by the fireplace.

He casts his eyes around the room. After sniffing the air, as though this were his first time in this house, his gaze drops to the ground. He notices, before I do, a trail of blood going from the parquet in the kitchen to the rug, and from the rug to my foot. What happened to your foot, he says. The reassurance vanishes from his voice. I just broke a glass in the kitchen, I must have stepped on the broken pieces when I came to open the door. He stands up. Before I can so much as blink, he has marched into the kitchen and returned with a cloth, cotton wool, and a bowl of water. He bends down in front of me. He lifts first one foot, then the other, cleaning each one with the damp cloth. One is fine, but he removes a jagged piece of glass from the side of the other. He cleans the cut and compresses it with the cotton wool. He brings me a pair of socks and my slippers from the bedroom. Aware of the pain in my ribs, he helps me put the socks on. Seeing that I'm still in my pajamas, he asks, Have you had breakfast? I got up late this morning, I haven't eaten anything yet. In that case let's go out, the fresh air will do you good. Out? He means the out that I looked at last night after getting out of the ambulance, when I stood in the gardens of the apartment block and saw the sky shrouded by hazy light, and the balconies. I can't place myself anywhere in the world I have seen once, the remainder of which I attempt to piece together with what little information I have in my head. If someone told me I was in a dream I'd believe them. Last night I dreamt that everything was rippling, as though floating in water, and flowing back and forth. Records, paintings, voices, faces, names. Nothing stays still, and nothing touches anything else. It isn't clear which era the objects are from. Are the singers whose pictures I saw on the album covers alive or dead? Are the people whose names I remember living, or have they remained in bygone eras? I'd better not go out today, I say, using the cut on my foot as an excuse. Okay, I'll just nip out and get a few things from the grocery store. After he has cleaned the broken glass in the kitchen and had a quick look inside the fridge, he goes out. Because Bek has a place in the outside world where he belongs, going out isn't an issue for him. Whereas I regard even my own face in the mirror as a stranger. I'm like a blank sheet of paper. I have no inside and no outside. My east and west are hazy, as are my south and north. No matter where I step, I feel as though I am about to tumble into a void. I spend my days waiting for night to fall. After I have taken my medicine with a glass of water I close my eyes, hoping my past will come back to me while I am asleep; I start counting. Forty-one, forty-two, forty-three.... I wonder if the directions, the names and paintings in my past existence are all in the right place. Was I in the right place in the past?

Bek, who returns laden with groceries and shows me each item before putting it away in the cupboard so I'll remember it, serves breakfast on the table in the lounge. He tells me I like fried eggs. Cheese, olives, tomatoes, honey, beef salami. He pours tea. As he waxes lyrical about the beautiful weather outside, as though describing a holiday resort, he keeps a close eye on my food preferences. Our band members phoned just now while I was in the grocery store, they want to see you. I thought it would do you good to go out with them. I said let's all go to Theodora's Tavern tomorrow night. You must be dying for a drink. He laughs. I turn my head and look at the bottles in the wooden cabinet. I must be a heavy drinker, look, the cabinet's full. No, you never overdo it. You're an occasional drinker, who savors the taste. You can hold your drink. Unlike me, who gets legless every time. Last month we went to Theodora's Tavern again for some food and drinks, and when I got legless you were the one who took me home. I sang belly-dance music to the taxi driver. Really? I'd love to be able to remember that. There's no need for you to remember it Boratin, I'll give you a repeat performance. He laughs again. He didn't laugh once when he visited me in the hospital. There he had seemed more upset than I was, whereas here he seems happier than I am. If I ever manage to catch up with my past I'll feel very close to him, I'll believe in him as well as in myself. Bek, I say, did I choose and buy the furniture in this house? You bought some of it, but you inherited most of it from your landlady. How long have I lived in this house? You moved in three years ago. We came to see it together. You liked the views of Beyazıt Tower and the lighthouse from the balcony. The landlady liked you too, she said you reminded her of her grandson, and let you have it there and then. She was an elderly Greek lady. She was moving out to go and live with her son because she was too old to live by herself.

I look at the figurine of Mary and Jesus on the mantelpiece. I know their names, but can't remember my landlady's. Mary isn't crying. The look on her face is sorrowful but tranquil at the same time. The sorrow is hers, but she has borrowed the tranquility from the lifeless face of her son lying in her arms. Should we think of that as life's greatness, or life's inconsistency? Bek, how long has that figurine been there? That figurine, he says, it was there when you moved in, your landlady left it, like she left a lot of things. Did I ever take any notice of it before? No, this is the first time I've ever heard you mention it, as far as you're concerned it's just a simple ornament, that's it. Simple? If I knew the kinds of things I used to care about before, then I'd have a much easier job working out what kind of person I am. Does anyone live here with me, I don't even know that. No, there's no one else Boratin, you live alone. Have I always lived alone? Last year a girl moved in with you for a few months, but since she left you've lived by yourself. Where is she now, did we split up? Yes, after you broke up she packed her bags and left Istanbul. I stop dead when I hear that. It takes me more by surprise than learning that I was a musician in my previous life, or that I'm from a wealthy family. How did I take the break up, would you say my ending up like this had anything to do with the girl? No, I doubt it. You weren't too cut up about finishing with her. You didn't write a single verse about her, you didn't feel the need to pour your heart out when we were out drinking. You've moved on. How have I moved on, like the Mary in that figurine? As Mary clutches her son in her arms, her lips are tightly sealed. All her words are stashed inside her marble mouth. I've been staring at her all morning, I can't take my eyes off her. Her face is beautiful, the turn of her neck, her gaze, the expression on her lips. Beauty sits on her face like the purest form of truth. As these thoughts run through my mind, I have no idea what to believe. And what I am most suspicious of is time. I don't know if Mary is still alive. I wonder if death eventually freed her too of all her troubles. It's been a long time, says Bek, they lived two thousand years ago. Nowadays they're part of a religious legend. To confirm the size of past time to myself, I think about numbers. So, it's been as long as all that, I say, doesn't time fly. Bek gives me an odd look. It's the first time I have seen an expression on his face that's neither concern nor happiness. I ask if I'm interested in religion. Religion? No, you're interested in art, in music. You don't believe in anything else. You play the guitar and sing and leave everyone in Istanbul's blues bars openmouthed. You're the best member of our band by a long shot. We only play with you so we can complement your songs and be an appendage of yours. I'm not just saying that to make you feel better. You know that, as a nation, we either praise someone to the heavens or drag their name through the mud. Do we? Yes, there's no in-between. But I'm telling you the honest truth Boratin, you're a brilliant singer and songwriter.

I stare at the records and the multicolored guitars. I would be just as fascinated if they were fishing lines, or blunt axes, worn out with use. If they took me to a different house and said I was a fisherman or a woodcutter, I'd accept that too. People's past fate can be anything under the sun. Who knows when I put up the record covers on the wall. Delta Blues. I wonder why the Submarine cover underneath them is handwritten and not the original print. That's the name of our band Boratin. You've been working on our first album for some time. You did the lettering on the album cover yourself and put it up there. I realize that Bek believes in me, and not only that, he loves me. And he desperately wants me to believe in him too, and to be the person he wants me to be. He tops up our tea glasses. He takes his cigarette packet out of his pocket and lights one. He's curious to see if I'll take one too. I don't hesitate. I pull out a cigarette and light it. The first drag leaves a bitter taste in my throat, but the second feels good. Bek smiles. I wish I'd told you you don't smoke, he says. You might not have touched them. You mustn't rush when it comes to life Boratin. To tell you the truth, there's nothing worth rushing for. Just let it flow, and meanwhile, do whatever takes your fancy. I'll always be with you. I'll help you. For example. . . . Bek takes a drag from his cigarette and thinks. The list of things he could help me with must be long, or maybe quite the opposite, there might not be all that much to be done. Tomorrow, he says, let's sort out one or two things. Your credit cards and your mobile phone are unusable. Let's go to the bank and get you some new cards. We'll get you a new phone. I can't follow his next sentences. He talks about the cards and numbers and institutions I'll need so I can have an existence outside this house, in the street. Since this morning I've been under the impression that a guitar and a bottle of wine, plus my medicine, were all a person like me (what kind of person is that?) needed to live. Nothing else. I don't want anything from anyone and I don't want anyone to want anything from me. Whoever knows where I live can come and see me whenever they like, anyone who feels like it can telephone me. Boratin, your landline is working, isn't it? I phoned you but you didn't pick up. Was it you who phoned? Yes, it's only ever me or your sister who phone you on your landline. My sister? Yes. I turn my head and look at my phone sparkling in its wrought gold holder, looking as though it's about to ring at any moment. I am overcome by an inexplicable surge of pity, when I haven't even felt pity for myself for the past week. There was more than one call this morning, my sister must have been the other caller. Boratin, this telephone was here when you moved in. Because everyone uses mobiles no one's got a landline anymore. You didn't have yours disconnected because your sister prefers phoning you on your landline.

# Like a Spider That Doesn't Leave Its Web

# 4

As I trudge slowly up the street, I overhear a young man and woman walking ahead of me talking about death and happiness. If you want to be happy, says the woman, you need to find something to commit to, a belief, or a lover. But if you want to find truth, then follow death. The man and woman both have hair that comes down to their ears, cut straight. They're wearing identical boots and watches. Their voices sound the same, like twins. They stop when they come to the door of a secondhand book dealer. They remove their sunglasses and hang them from their top buttonholes. The plaster in the bookseller's is peeling and everywhere the paint on the wooden cornices is cracked. The shop window hasn't been cleaned in a long time. Compared to all the other buildings, this shop, which no one would give a second look, is old. The letters on its signboard have worn away. With a dusty record player, an old gramophone with a broken tonearm, and some randomly scattered books fading in the window in the autumn sunshine, a spider's web hanging snugly in the top corner of the window looks like the newest item in the shop.

The two young people enter and greet the book dealer with the warmth of people who know one another. After a few minutes of small talk, they check their wristwatches. Were they early, or late? The book dealer glances at a wall clock framed in wood and realizes it has stopped. He looks first at the hour hand, then at the minute hand, goes to the wall, and opens the door of the clock case. He asks the young pair what time it is, it's ten to three, adjusts the clock to the right time, and turns the winding crank. He steps back and surveys it as though admiring a valuable painting. The clock is working. I too step softly over the threshold. I greet the people inside. Instead of the clock I look at the books on the shelves. Take your time browsing, says the book dealer, if you need any help give me a shout. Okay, I say. I don't know why I came in here. Perhaps it was the young pair's conversation that intrigued me, or maybe I wanted to see what a secondhand book dealer's looked like. The book dealer turns around and shuffles back behind his counter. He rolls up his shirtsleeves. He spreads out a velvet cloth on the dusty counter. He straightens out the creases with the palms of his hands. He opens the drawer of a cabinet beside him. He takes out a book and places it on the velvet cloth. The book's striking, worn cover brings to mind a rare piece of fragile antique porcelain. He dons his glasses. Lovingly, he runs his fingers over the book. If every secondhand book dealer spends an entire lifetime awaiting just one book, and all the books he has acquired over the days and years only gain significance once it arrives, then this book dealer looks as though he has been united with that one book. The one that everyone has spent their whole lives dreaming about since the fall of the empire. Hunters—knowing that rare books lay scattered alongside dispersed families and ruined mansions, under the dust of the empire that collapsed years ago (how many years ago?)—frittered away lifetimes yearning for books that were often mentioned in newspapers but somehow never found. They even sullied their hands with blood for the sake of those books. For example, the handwritten *The Sky with the Sun at Its Center*, said to have been destroyed in the fire of the Library of Alexandria; or *Methods for Curing Lovesickness*, the last Sanskrit copy of which is presumed to have been in a caravan that was raided on the Silk Road; or *Endless Laughter*, which threw its readers into fits of laughter before they had even finished reading it, causing them to die in agony. All copies save one were consequently collected and burned by order of Queen Marguerite of Navarre, who had only one conserved in the treasure chamber. I believe that what I have before me now is a book of that caliber, says the book dealer, a work without equal.

The young pair moves closer to the counter, they stroke the velvet cloth but, fearful of damaging the book, keep a deferential distance from it. The beauty of a book, says the book dealer, lies in the fact that no other book can arouse the same feelings in you. That's why you can't compare good books. Not wanting to keep them in suspense any longer, the book dealer starts to read the first page. As he reads, the young pair gaze at the book up close, transfixed, as if they alone have had the good fortune to uncover a wondrous secret. They listen with hunched shoulders and outstretched necks. They forget about the outside world, as though the sight of their reflections in a lake has paralyzed them, their hair almost brushing against invisible water. They had heard that in the beginning was the Word, now they can hear from the book dealer's voice that in the end too there will only be the Word. Life is comprehending the word. And when the book dealer's slow-moving lips eventually say that death too consists of words, the young pair raise their heads and gape at him. If a book states that on the very first page, who knows what promises all the other pages might contain. When I hear that death consists of a single word, I slip out the door quietly. They don't notice me. I stand in front of the shop. I contemplate my reflection in the window. If I could detect a stirring in my face, or a twitch in my eye, I would be able to decide what to think. Everyone needs a past it seems, and now everyone is trying to create one for me. The past is like a train that grows distant and vanishes into the darkness. If you don't remember where you traveled on it and which stations you got off at, then you won't know who you are either. Why am I standing in the middle of this street instead of in some other country, and why is the body I'm gazing at in the shop window this age, rather than some other age? This is my body, with its wavy hair and broad shoulders. It's no one else's. I know that. I may have doubts about the phone in my house or the guitars lined up in a row, but I have no doubts about this body. It's the only asset I possess. I run my hands through my hair. These hands are mine, they move when I want and lie still when I want. My eyes see the world, my ears hear the noises in the street. I feel hungry. My broken rib frequently makes its presence felt. While my past abandons me and my mind gets off that train and stands by itself, my body stays faithful to me. It isn't just now that my body is mine, it was mine before, I have no doubt about that. I have a past that this body carried. I move closer to my image in the shop window. When I notice the crowd reflected in it, I turn and look behind me. People are walking up and down the street. The atmosphere is lively and bustling, like a bird market. The sound of telephones. Different ringtones. I place my hand in my shirt pocket and touch the new phone that I bought from a vendor this morning. I look at a young couple walking by me, then at a woman in a flowery skirt holding her son's hand.

I have been out since this morning. Hesitantly treading the streets of Istanbul. I study the faces I see entering and exiting state buildings, banks, shops. The cars racing past me and the people rubbing shoulders with me in the crowd make me uneasy. I had assumed that everyone in the street would pity me and look at me with compassion, as they had in the hospital. But no one even notices me. It's clear that the officials' smiles, the ink in the signatures scrawled on paper, the people who look identical in the silence of the queues in front of glass doors, all carry different worlds inside them; perhaps they are waiting for the sound of a train that will wake them one night. As I walk up the street behind the woman with the flowery skirt and her son, I wonder if the fortunate or the unfortunate people in this street are in the majority. Which of the two am I closest to? The good fortune of having jumped off the Bosphorus Bridge and stayed alive, or the ill fortune of having lost my memory? On my last night in the hospital, the patient in the next bed said the opposite: Maybe you're unfortunate to still be alive and fortunate to have lost your memory. The boy walking in front of me drops his biscuit. His mother bends down and picks it up. They take a left turn. When I follow them onto the street, I find myself suddenly emerging into a square, in front of the Galata Tower. The moment I see it I realize it's the Galata Tower. Was it a place where I used to come often in the past? All the tables in the nearby cafés and restaurants are full. The autumn sunshine is generous. I can feel several eyes in the crowd on me. Boratin! Boratin! When I turn and look I see a flustered Bek running towards me. Where did you disappear to, he says, I went into a shop to get some cigarettes, I thought you were waiting outside.

## 5

Bek, what was I like before, what sort of person was I, what did I look like? If you're talking about your weight, you were always this size. Your hair used to be shorter, then you started growing it. We can go to the hairdresser's today if you like, then I can get a haircut and shave as well. Okay, didn't I have any distinguishing scars, or illnesses, or did I ever have any plastic surgery...? What are you on about Boratin, you're the envy of everyone in town. Didn't you see the way the woman serving you at the bank was looking at you? Even though I was the one talking to her, she couldn't take her eyes off you. When she asked for your phone number I don't think she was interested in adding it to your account details, she looked as though she was planning to phone you after work. If she doesn't you can always go back to the bank one day.

Boratin's face remains expressionless. Shall we go and get a drink, he says. Okay, but let's sort out your business first. What business? Don't you remember you said you wanted to buy an alarm clock? Don't worry if you've forgotten, we all have our little lapses. I don't know what you want it for anyway, the last thing you need is an alarm clock. Right now you don't need to wake up, you need to sleep. Pull yourself together a bit first, then I'll buy you one. Boratin looks at the watchseller's shop on the other side of the square. He makes no move to cross over. He turns his head and glances at the buildings on the right. Their facades are painted in different colors. Which one looks the best? The ice-blue four-story building reminds him of the color of one of the guitars at home. On the ground floor there's a café with tables spilling out into the square. Boratin starts walking towards one of them. As he sits down, he realizes he's tired. From trudging up streets. It's going to take time to acclimatize to the city. I mustn't rush, he thinks. Like the spider in the book dealer's shop window, he should wait for everything to come to him without leaving his web, the past included. People look at life in the same way as they look at books in a book dealer's shop. New books are cheap, old ones expensive. In life too, old time is important. It's yesterday that's valuable, not today, and the day before that even more so. That's why they're trying to give Boratin a past. If he said, I don't understand. If he asked, if I'm here today I may also be here tomorrow, but how can I exist yesterday? They would look at him with pity. They would offer him explanations. Their coffees arrive quickly. As Bek adds sugar and stirs his coffee, he examines him out of the corner of his eye. Boratin doesn't touch the sugar, he raises the cup to his lips slowly and takes a sip. He likes the strong taste in his mouth, he takes another sip. Does it matter how he drank his coffee in the past? Today he likes, is able to like it, like this. If he used to take sugar in his coffee but now prefers it without sugar, what conclusions should he draw from that? He can't make any sense of his mind. Do we have any other errands left? he asks Bek. We've bought you a new phone, we've applied for a credit card, we've got you a new ID to replace the one that got damaged in the water. Bek counts the completed errands on his fingers. When he gets to his fourth finger, he says, Your driver's license is unusable too, we'll sort that out tomorrow. Why do I need a driver's license, have I got a car? No, but you sometimes borrow my motorbike and go out for a spin. It's only then that Boratin notices the two boys and two girls standing beside the motorbikes parked on the other side of the square. He imagines himself as being like them. Maybe he used to jump on his motorbike and come here with his friends. Maybe he used to drink standing up, like them, rest his head on the shoulder of the girl next to him, grab the bottle out of her hand and take a swig. He was getting ready to hit the road. In a moment he would put on his sunglasses, sit the girl behind him on the motorbike, bow his head slightly and drive into the wind. Nothing would matter, except experiencing that moment. The girl with her arms around his waist would lean her body against his. They were being transported by pure speed. The world would flow by them on both sides, painted in hazy colors.

They order another coffee. Are we both the same age? asks Boratin. Yes, says Bek, we've turned twenty-eight. It doesn't matter that you didn't know how old you were when the woman in the bank asked. When someone asks me out of the blue like that I sometimes have to stop and rack my brain too. What would you do in my position, says Boratin, I mean if you forgot your past? I would trust you Boratin. As long as you were beside me I'd follow you and your memory. That's what we normally do anyway. We listen to what others remember and compare it with what we know, and quite often we realize there are gaps in our mind and things we've got wrong. I've been thinking about your predicament for the past few days, and it doesn't strike me as all that scary. Everyone goes out of their way to live without a past anyway. Look at all these people, sitting at tables, walking through the square. They live as though they have no yesterday, as though they only belong to today. Boratin looks at the faces in the square. He turns his head and examines the people sitting at the neighboring tables. When his gaze alights on the far end of the café, he meets the eye of a woman sitting by herself several tables away. They haven't made eye contact by chance. He notices her unblinking eyes staring at him. She knows him, she's staring resolutely, as though she's been sitting there waiting for this moment from the start. Her hair is long, her eyebrows are long, the fingers holding her cigarette are long. She looks the same age as him. As she takes a drag from her cigarette and exhales the smoke, the expression on her face changes. Her eyes become more hostile. She exposes her teeth between her slightly quivering lips. There are things she wants to say. He can see that from the tension in her lips. Boratin averts his eyes and turns to look ahead of him. He reaches over to the packet in Bek's hand and takes a cigarette. He flicks on the lighter. Is a person's past like this woman? Its eyes bore into you night and day. Her face is attractive, her gaze is confident and, for some reason, angry. You know it's there even if you don't turn and look. You focus on the people and the sounds passing in front of you, but your mind is held by the gaze behind you. No matter how fast you move, it will be there behind you. When you surreptitiously turn your head, you see it, it's there. While it is certain of what it's going to do, you have no idea. Bek, you say, do you know the woman sitting at the back, at the table near the wall? You both look together. The woman has turned her face away, she's talking on the phone. She's twiddling a lock of her hair with one hand. No I don't, says Bek, why do you ask? She was just looking at us, or maybe I just imagined it. Since the morning I had quickly grown used to nobody in the street seeing me, or turning and looking at my face. I found it bewildering now to come eye to eye with someone. I'd love it if no eye could touch me. If I never felt anyone's gaze on my back. If I could walk into any street I liked and sit anywhere I wanted, when I wanted. If the perfume of the women walking past me smelled familiar, but none of them turned and looked at me. If they did I have no idea what I would do. If they greeted me and asked how I was, what would I say? I'm sorry, I've lost my memory, I don't know who you are. Maybe I'll remember you next time we meet. Until then you must bear in mind that, even if you haven't forgotten me, I've forgotten you. Tell our common acquaintances. So they'll realize how serious things are. I don't want anyone to be offended by my blank expression, or to stare after me and make me uneasy. How did it happen? I don't know any more than you do. I opened my eyes, I'm nobody. I have a body. That's all. I read my name on my half-destroyed ID card. I watched my face in the mirror. I looked at the covers of the records I've collected. What did I feel when I looked at them before? What if I'll never know? Or what if I thought it was all a dream. If, when I woke up, I told the people around me that I dreamed I was friends with someone who went by the odd name of Bek and that a woman with long hair was watching me, but I didn't remember them. And we all laughed together. If I said I was a blues singer (blues?) and that I was just as famous for my good looks as I was for my voice and we laughed some more. There's no past in dreams. In dreams people only live that moment, they're not aware of the past. This is me.

I turn and look at the woman behind me. I try to look for some meaning in her eyes. She turns her head, raises her hand, and asks the waiter for the bill. She takes out her purse. She tosses her phone, her cigarette packet, and her lighter in her bag. It's a bit hot here, I say to Bek, shall we go? We too pay our bill. We walk down the street on the corner of the square, going back the way we came. Yüksek Kaldırım has become even more congested. There's different music blaring out of every shop. A child on a street corner is selling water from a bucket filled with bottles. Cold, ice cold water. A man who looks like a writer strolls through the crowd in an overcoat and felt hat. He walks along the cobbled road holding a book. He stops for breath when he reaches the book dealer's I was just in. While straightening his hat he glances at the old books in the shop window. Then he looks at his watch. Unlike me, he has no trouble differentiating between one year ago and a hundred years ago. I bump into someone walking past me. I stumble. The pain in my rib smarts. I stop and take deep breaths. Are you all right? asks Bek. Yes, I'm fine. I'm trying not to lose sight of the long-haired woman walking a few paces ahead. I keep her within range. Loud laughter pours out of a café on the left. The happiness of the group—quite clearly tourists— sitting on the kilim-upholstered armchairs pervades the street. We've been to this café together a few times, says Bek, the burgers here are delicious. Do you fancy something to eat? No, I say, let's walk around a bit first, then we can eat.

I cast a look at the crowd growing before our eyes. When I fail to see the long-haired woman, I realize I've lost her. The woman, swept along by the tide, leaves just as she arrived. She wasn't in my life and now she vanishes completely. My eyes scour the streets in vain. Shops selling musical instruments, sign painters, döner kebab restaurants. People come out of one and head inside another. There's a mysterious happiness in this crowd. A happiness that's unknown to me. Maybe it's unknown to them too. When we reach the avenue at the end of the street, the roar of cars drowns out every other sound. We walk past old men selling tissues, and down-and-out buskers playing the *saz*. Like everyone else, we skirt two meters around the sleeping dog sprawled out in the street, to avoid disturbing it. We turn the corner at a gray building with solid walls. There, a sea bursting out of its mold appears before us. It's indigo blue. Cold. I didn't know the sea was so close. It thrashes from Galata Bridge to the Bosphorus, and from there towards the Marmara. A leaping wave crashes to the shore and spreads out on the cobblestones, seeping into the soil through the cracks. The blue of the sea, broken stones, soil. I take a step back. I reach over and take Bek's arm. I tug him along with me, as though we're rushing to get somewhere. I stride past the benches. I turn onto the street opposite the quay. Once on the narrow street, the sound of the waves abates, as does the wind. I slow down. The ferry must be due, people are scuttling towards the quay. They are racing to catch the last hours of a day that is practically over. Everyone is in a hurry. The ferry is about to leave. I bump into someone again. I must have a habit of bumping into people. I need to learn how to walk in a crowd all over again. I stand aside to give way. It's the long-haired woman. She's staring at me in disbelief. Fool, she whispers, you fool. She whips her sunglasses off the top of her head, puts them on and sweeps past angrily. Bek touches me on the shoulder, Are you all right? he asks. Yes, I say, I think so. Roaming the streets all day has tired me out. I don't think I'll go out to meet our friends tonight. I can see them another time. I'd better go home and rest.

## 6

Bek takes me home. He's worried because I won't let him stay with me tonight either. See you, he says. Bye, I reply. I'm talking to myself inside a circle. Ever since I've been home I've been repeating the same resolution: I'm not going to force myself to think about the past. That's what I say, but then I can't do anything but worry about it. It's like telling someone who wakes up in the dark not to look at it. Wherever he turns it's dark, if he closes his eyes it's still dark. Far away, in the depths of infinity, light has not yet appeared. Can the opposite of dark be sound instead of light? The sound of this house. The sound of the bell. The sound of music. I look at the album covers on the wall. I go and sit beside the record collection. I run my fingers over the records. I select a record and examine its cover. Then another, and another. I know all the singers on the covers, but I don't remember when or where I bought them. I chance upon a Bessie Smith album. Her lips are parted in the cover photograph, she's smiling as though she wants to give me some of her breath. I cover her mouth with my hand. I keep it there until my hand starts sweating. When I take it away I notice that she's still smiling at me. I take the record out of its sleeve. I'm not sure how I should hold it. After turning it between my fingers, I place it on the record player and press ON. I lift the needle. The record wobbles as it rotates. And crackles when I lower the needle onto it. A piano starts to play. A piano with worn keys, covered in an unholy amount of dust. Bessie Smith's throaty voice spills out. *I've got the blues. I feel so lonely. I'll give the world if I could only make you understand.* I understand the lyrics. Which must mean I know English. And I also know that it's English she's singing in. I lie on my back in the middle of the living room. *'Cause when you're gone, I'm worried all day long....* I stretch my arms out. The coolness of the floor flows from my back to my chest. Outside, evening is approaching fast. Anyone can sense the full moon rising even without looking out the window. There is a faint breeze in the street. There are piles of rubbish heaped up by dark walls. The sound of laughter comes through an open window. A young couple are kissing on a street corner. They have no money in their pockets and no room to go to. A man appears on the opposite sidewalk, he stops and lights a cigarette. The dogs accompanying him stop too. Anyone walking alone at this time of night should either smoke a cigarette or have a drink, and find a corner to curl up in before midnight strikes. I hear whistling. The whistler is a young man sitting under the streetlamp a bit farther up the road. He's obviously waiting for someone. Occasionally he turns his head to see if there's anyone coming from the other end. He's whistling a Bessie Smith song. I can't tell if it's happy or sad. Images form in my mind as I listen to the song, but I don't feel anything. One lifeless apparition follows another, people and sounds merge into the night. I listen to the song without any joy or nostalgia. What did I feel in the past? *Baby won't you please come home, Baby won't you please come home....* Something's ringing. I turn my head and look. It's the phone.

I reach over to the faded coffee table for the phone that looks older than I am. I lift the receiver and place it on my ear. A distant humming that reminds me of the mechanical sound of cables. The cables, that at this moment are transmitting who knows how many thousands of voices, in who knows how many thousands of houses, quiver and echo. I wait for a voice to reach me. When I don't hear anything I place the receiver on my other ear. Boratin, says a woman. Her voice is throaty, like Bessie Smith's. That's why it sounds familiar. Abla, I say. Yes my love, it's me. After that there might be silence. Or, she might speak and I might just make noises of approval. Are you there Boratin? Yes Abla, I'm here. That's the only thing I know. I'm here, inside an apartment I don't know. Boratin, I've been trying to get a hold of you for days. Are you inundated with concerts again? What if I said, Abla, I don't know you? What if I said, if I saw you in the street I wouldn't recognize you? Instead I say, Abla, I'm really busy, I'm usually out all day and I get back late. You're in Istanbul Boratin, that's enough to wear anyone out. Just seeing it in films makes my hair stand on end, even from this distance. You're young and you don't look after yourself. It was the same when you were little, you'd go out to play marbles and forget all about dinner, you'd spend all day chasing after a ball in the street until evening. Then you got hooked on the guitar. My sister says the same thing every time she phones me. I can tell by her calm voice. Every phone call features examples from my childhood. Remembering the past gives her joy. She loves giving me affectionate warnings. Don't go neglecting your health and getting ill. No Abla, I'm not that careless. Talking to my sister is a game. I get the hang of it straightaway. Is this what life is? If I'm going to live out the rest of my days and years playing games like these.... You say you're not careless, but don't forget that time last spring when you stayed out in the rain and got ill. I have forgotten. One day I hope I'll be able to tell my sister that. When you were a child, she says, you would get so engrossed in whatever you were playing, you would stay outside in the rain. Would I? I think of a child in a small town growing up in the rain. I remember rain from books and films but I don't know what it looks like. That child is as happy as children in films, until he realizes there are other lives in the world, and that he can reach them. No one can rein him in. He can feel the whip of dreams flogging his back. He wants to make time go faster, to make life flow at top speed, to make the roads ahead of him clear. And, when the time comes, to go away. Was that the kind of child I was? How did I get a yearning for the guitar in a small town? I push the question away. How are you Abla, is everyone well? We're well, I can't complain, you know, seeing neighbors and that. One of our lodgers is leaving, I've found a new one, he's moving in next month. Aladdin drafted and wrote the contract all by himself. He's grown huge since you last saw him. I listen to my sister's words carefully, trying to work out who Aladdin is. Well done Aladdin, I say, he's grown that big then. What do I think I'm doing? Oh yes, Uncle Boratin, you should see how tall he's grown.... It's been such a long time since I've seen him Abla, time flies so quickly. Yes, it's been three years, it just flows by like water. Every summer Aladdin dreams that you'll come and spend the holiday with him. Are you counting the years? Well, the last time you came was to your brother-in-law's funeral. With time Aladdin has gotten used to his father not being around, he's pinned all his hopes on you now. He's so happy when you send him presents, when he's opening them he asks, when is my uncle coming? Just recently he's started to sing songs, just like you. He plants a chair in front of the mirror and sits and sings for hours. And do you know what, his voice sounds like yours. I haven't been to see my sister and my fatherless nephew for all these years. What sort of a person am I, or rather, what sort of a person was I? I'm going to come, I say, just let me get some of this work out of the way and I'll come and see you. The words pop out of my mouth. Do you mean it, are you really coming? She's so delighted it's obvious I've never said anything like that before. Three years that pass without seeing a sister. Yes, I have a handful of concerts, but after that I'll come and stay with you for a while. Come Boratin, I've missed you so much. When you were at university you used to come every month. In those days I used to tell you not to come so often, I didn't want you to miss your classes. I couldn't bear to think of you traveling for twelve hours. Did it take twelve hours Abla? You see, it's been so long since you've been here, you can't even remember the way. In those days you used to tell me the journey wasn't tiring. You would get the night train from Haydarpaşa Station and be at Nehirce the next morning. It made me so happy when you suddenly showed up at the door. Every time you came you'd say, Nehirce hasn't changed. I don't know if it was reproach or satisfaction that I could detect in your voice, but you'd say it with a little smile. Oh,

I would ask, and does Istanbul change then? Yes, you would say, it does, along with everything and everyone in it. What you see today might not be there tomorrow, and in the evening you may say that what you believed in the morning is a lie. Everyone trains their soul accordingly. Is Istanbul still changing Boratin? I don't know what to say. If I told her Istanbul hasn't changed for several days, that it's stuck in a never-ending moment, she wouldn't believe me. Lies and the truth are one now. Right and wrong are the same. Mosques built from stone and steel skyscrapers look as though they're the same age. Istanbul has stopped, I've stopped. I got lost at the time gate separating old and new. I'm searching for a word to believe in. I think the dead are still alive, maybe I'm under the impression that a lot of the living are dead. My mind is a graveyard where the living and the dead lie wrapped in each other's arms. The stench of rotten meat mixes with the most tantalizing perfumes. Who is the one speaking, who is the one groaning, who is the one who's going to wake up the next morning and go to work? When the telephone rings who is going to reach over and pick up the receiver, speak, grow anxious? If my mind was this convoluted when I was a small child still living in Nehirce, my sister will know. One day I'll be able to ask her. I'll be able to find out if I have a past I might wish to return to. If I left and haven't been back except for funerals, is it entirely my fault? A Nehirce that can't win my affection can't be all that perfect. Boratin are you there?

I'm like water seeping out of a broken cup. I can't return to my cup, and if I did, it wouldn't be able to contain me. My fate is to want to sleep and not be able to, to read the names in my address book over and over again and not be able to remember them, and to wake up every day and stare at the endless contours of the wall. If there is a God (is there?) It plays a different game of fate with each of Its mortals. And this is the one that's fallen to me. The songs on the record don't shed any light. Images are lifeless, I can't touch them. I can't feel what I do touch. I can't understand what I feel. There is a way out, it's out there somewhere, waiting, but every morning I start the day without knowing what I'm going to do. Boratin, darling? As I listen to my sister, Bessie Smith's face swims before my eyes. She's smiling benevolently, as though she wants to give me some of her breath.

# You Shouldn't Always Take the Same Route Home

## 7

The beams streaming in through the venetian blinds cast a dim light into the doctor's consulting room. The kilim designs on the sofa cover come to life. The scent of the cat that was wandering around just now but has since disappeared into the next room lingers on the sofa. The same scent pervades the armrests of the armchair I'm sitting on. Do I have a scent? Aware that my attention is straying, the doctor hands me a glass of water. She waits for me to drink it, then continues talking. The taxi you took was crossing over to the European side via the Bosphorus Bridge. When an accident brought the traffic to a halt, you opened your eyes in the back seat where you had dozed off, looked outside, and tried to work out where you were. According to the taxi driver. If there hadn't been an accident the taxi would have carried on driving and you would have carried on sleeping. After a few minutes the driver got out of the taxi to find out what had caused the traffic jam; the cars were at a standstill, so he phoned a friend. While he was chatting you got out of the car and walked to the edge of the bridge. The buzz of the city. The sea shimmering with the city lights. Background noise. Apparently you stuck your head over the bridge and looked down, into the sea. But only the moment before, you had wanted to go home. That's what you said to the driver when you got into the taxi. That night's concert had been a great success. You had been swept along with the crowd's excitement. Do you mind me telling you all this? We need to talk about it, even if you don't remember. I've read articles about you, and interviews. You cited Kurt Cobain and Yavuz Çetin as your favorite musicians. Both of them committed suicide. The doctor looks at the glass in my hand, to try and determine whether I want more water. She watches the movements of my fingers. I'm thinking about what she said in our last session, about my mother and father both dying in a car accident. The glass is empty. It disappears in my hand. If I squeeze it just a bit harder it will break. Apparently the active ingredient in the drugs I'm taking is lithium. Lithium unburdens the mind and frees it of obsessive questions. It seems I won't need to fret about anything anymore. If the past has abandoned me then I too can abandon the past, until it comes back of its own accord. I don't want to think about all this. I don't care if jumping into water is an indication of the desire to return to the mother's womb and jumping from a height is an indication of a creative urge. My mind is on other things. Doctor, when I opened my eyes in the hospital I asked you what had happened to me. What did happen to me? But you asked me who I was. Who was I? I could hear ferries' horns. The sound of a ferry in the midst of the commotion in the street. Did a sound that slipped

away from the din and reached my ears have any significance as far as life was concerned? You were asking me
my name, but I was trying to remember why I wanted to
die. Knowing one didn't make the answer to the other
any easier. What brings on the desire to die? The ferries'
horns echoed inside my head. Car horns, the cries of
street peddlers. But there was no sound of seagulls. It's a
special skill our mind has, to think about what isn't there,
you said. Doctor, I wish everyone forgot the past, I wish
everyone went to bed at night and woke up with an empty
mind and didn't look at me with such pity. Boratin Bey,
if that were the case then the world would be different,
human nature would become something else. That's what
I'm saying Doctor, maybe then no one would end their
life for no reason. The words fly before my eyes, floating
like leaves, gliding in the air, first in one direction, then
another. I catch the words nearest me, shove them into
my mouth, and spout them out without chewing. This
morning as I was leaving home the grocer on the corner
saw me and ran up to me. He had heard what had happened to me. When he saw me alive and well, he beamed
and said, You got off lightly, as though I had been in a
trifling little accident. He took my hand between his two
hands and squeezed it warmly. He called over his daughter, who appeared in the shop's doorway, and told her to
kiss my hand. I stopped her. She was about thirteen or
fourteen. With a shy expression. She had passed her exam
(which exam?). The grocer squeezed my hand again and

thanked me. He said that thanks to my help the girl had passed her exam and saved her life. Did I give her lessons, or pay for her to do some course? While the grocer was reeling off long sentences starting with, Thanks to your kindness, the girl bowed her head in embarrassment. Well done, you clever girl, I said. While on the one hand the thought that I was a good person was strangely comforting, on the other hand I was anxious to get away from this conversation that left me speechless. I realized once again that I wasn't certain of anything besides my body. Is there anyone who can be certain of anything besides their body? I take my medicine at night and wake up the next morning with fresh hope, but at the end of the day I find myself back in the same place. I sit on the edge of the bed and examine my hands, arms, and legs as though seeing them for the first time. What can be worth dying for? Was there anything that valuable in my life? I had fallen asleep in a taxi on the way home after a wonderful evening. When I woke up and found myself on the bridge I had tried to kill myself. If that is all life amounts to then maybe there's no point in dying for it.

The doctor takes the glass out of my hand. She realizes I'm looking at the mirror on the wall instead of at her. She waits for me to speak. After a long silence she asks, What can you see there? I see a mirror. Reflecting beams of light. The kilim designs on the sofa changing direction. The cat's scent pervading the mirror's interior. A drop of water on the edge of the empty glass. The din from the street drowning out the doctor's voice. Boratin Bey, will you tell me what you can see? I see a mirror. I don't mean that, I'm asking what you can see in the mirror, your face. My face? Yes, weren't you examining your face? Half this city would give their eyeteeth for such a handsome face. Instead of asking, what about the other half? I say, Are you really a doctor? She smiles. The journalists who praise you by likening your music to your face have a point. Those good looks alone are enough to live for. I turn back to the mirror. Just as I do every morning, I look without blinking. The image in the mirror doesn't blink either. I wait to see which of us will grow tired and give in. Whoever blinks first is me. When I stand in front of a mirror for a long time I get confused about which side I'm on. I think of the tale of the forty-leg centipede. The doctor reaches out and points at my fingers, as though she is going to touch them. These are the best guitar-playing fingers of recent years, she says. There are values in life that are worth living for Boratin Bey. If you say your body is the only thing you're certain of, that will do for a start. I look at my fingers. They're bony. Thin-veined. Why am I me? Why am I Boratin, and not a doctor, or a grocer? The answer to that isn't written on my ID or credit card. Why did my parents die in a car accident? An accident caused a bottleneck on the Bosphorus Bridge. Apparently I woke up and looked out the taxi window. It seems I thought my parents had died in the accident farther ahead. The years and the distance in between don't matter. The dead can always die again, at any time, in any place. And I can be born again (can I?). When I opened my eyes in the hospital you could have told me I was someone else, someone whose parents were still alive. You could have spared me my orphaned childhood. Words, words. Letters, numbers, but mostly question marks flutter before my eyes. I want to put a question mark even after the word yes. Yes? My whole life will pass like this. Do you know doctor, once there was a forty-leg centipede, with a perfect figure that no one could take their eyes off. He had a graceful walk, he was a good dancer. One day they asked him: Which leg do you use to take such elegant steps? Do you use your seventh right leg first, followed by your fourteenth left leg? And do you then raise your twenty-first right leg and place your thirty-second left leg on the ground? The forty-leg centipede realized that to that day he had never given a moment's thought to the steps he took. Intrigued, he started to walk, trying to work out which leg he raised, on which side. All his legs became entangled. Never mind dancing, he couldn't even manage to walk on a straight road. In my previous life, I too was bound by my habits, just like everyone else. When I lost my memory I was forced to think about details. The obligation to recall a time I don't remember. I stumble. I bump into people when I'm walking in the street. The calendar inside my head is all mixed up. I think we're living the old times now and that distant places are within easy reach. In my apartment there's a figurine of the statue of Mary and Jesus in Rome. When I look at it I see Rome inside the map of Istanbul. Jesus has just died. Mary, mourning in the dark streets, is begging for bread with the migrants. The speed of light has been calculated. All the continents have been discovered. Now the world is waiting for someone to discover a new habitable planet. I'm tired of remembering these details, of doubting every single one, then slotting each of them into the appropriate place, one by one. I'm incapable of walking in the street. I want to go home, lock the door, and be by myself. I'm afraid of myself. What if I am not me.... While I was in the hospital I watched a news report on television about a man who had escaped from prison. He used to lock people in a chamber under his house in Istanbul, tie their hands and feet behind them with rope, torture them, bury their bodies in the soil, then go up one floor and live an ordinary life with his wife and children. I wasn't amazed by how the man could have done all those things, but by how others could have lived with such a person, how they could have sat at the same table as him and slept in the same bed. After the man was captured he showed no remorse and said he had done it all in the name of God. Fifteen years. In prison terms, that's a long time. Perhaps the years taught him remorse. Then he escaped from prison. He thought the false ID in his pocket would allow him to escape from his past too. The outside world seemed foreign to him. It wasn't his old world. He woke up in the middle of the night, in a taxi stuck halfway across a bridge, with the urge to kill himself. He climbed up to the bridge's railings and held out his arms. He leapt up like a bird, his wings carried him down, to a sea beyond everyone's reach. Wasn't there a song about that? In my sick bed I thought, what if I'm that man. Your words and the reporter's words were the same distance away, Doctor. Everything was the same distance from my body. It was later on that I got to know the crowds in the city. I'm trying to get used to the noise. I have trouble getting words out. When I repeat a word too many times it loses its meaning. When I say I should sleep, the word *sleep* melts away. When I say my childhood, the word *child* crumbles, letter by letter. And when the letters join together again, their order changes and they become a new word. I don't understand that new word. Songs come to my mind. I decide to follow notes instead of letters. I hum a tune. But then the notes become scattered too. Each note that changes place appears in the wrong position. The song on my lips turns into a deafening racket.

8

Clutching a *simit*, I head into the center of the park and sit down on a bench. People chatting under trees, dozing in the shade. People lying on their backs, contemplating the sky. I raise my head to see where the seagulls are flying. In Istanbul it's customary to feed the seagulls *simit*; was it a custom I used to observe? I, I, I. In the old days (how old?) there was no *I* in the language people spoke. They didn't say, who am I, they asked, who is Boratin? Instead of saying, I'm hungry, they said, Boratin is hungry. Boratin is sitting in the park. Boratin is contemplating the sky. Boratin is thinking, but he doesn't want to think. He doesn't want to get up. He doesn't want to leave. But he doesn't know what he does want either. Now he is chewing slowly. He remembers this taste, even though it's the first time he's eating *simit*. The brain works in strange ways. It's got me in the palm of its hand, without saying a single word to me. Who belongs to whom, do I own my brain, or does my brain own me? The sound of a ferry's horn. If I stand up I'll be able to see the ferry. If I walk towards it I won't have to go to the sea, if I wave to the ferry from a distance. If I wave to the ferry, as is customary in Istanbul. If I whistle to the seagulls. Every ferry has its own flock of seagulls that follows it. When it's choppy, when it's windy. The passengers throw up pieces of *simit*, the seagulls cut through the air like knives and catch every morsel. While I sit on the bench, my brain has wandered off to the shore and is gazing at the ferry. It's tossing *simit* to the seagulls. I know that my brain lives by thinking. But I am not it. I am sitting in the park eating *simit*.

I see someone shuffling in my direction. I can tell by his face that he's coming towards me. He's around my age. With a thin mustache. Long legs. A raised shirt collar. Rolled-up sleeves. Hello, he says. Hello, I say. He sits beside me. He leans back on the bench. He takes a deep breath, puffs up his chest, then exhales. As though he has been carrying the entire burden of life on his shoulders. He casts his eyes around him, at the growing crowd. You can't trust these people, he says. I'm human too, right, but no one gives a damn about my troubles. Look at them. They're all sitting in their little groups. Don't imagine that just because they're sitting together they know each other. Most of them are strangers. If they got up and sat next to someone else, no one would care, they'd just pick up their conversation from where they had left off. It's just me they avoid. Anyone would think I was out to borrow money; I sit next to them, say a couple of words, and they get up and leave. The man falls silent. He raises his head. He seems more anxious and tense than I am. I realize he doesn't recognize me. How are you, I say, how's life? His expression becomes more gentle. He smiles. Life is the same as ever, he says, but I've made up my mind to change it. I've bought myself an engagement ring. Now I'm looking for the girl who's going to be my fiancée. Look. He holds out his hand and shows me his ring. It looks too big for his bony finger. His hand's shadow trembles along with his hand. We fit comfortably on the bench. Me, him, and our shadows. Was it the doctor who said our past is like a shadow, or did I think of it myself in my previous life? Our past is always with us, apparently. No matter how many years pass, it's always the same distance away from us, like a shadow. I introduce myself and ask his name. He says, Serka. How will you find the girl who's going to be your fiancée, Serka? I say. I go to that shopping center opposite the park, he says. He points. I see the building beyond the trees, on the other side of the road. I go there every day, he says, to search the shops and cafés for my fiancée. Then I come here. The park gets crowded in the afternoons. Yesterday I thought a woman I saw here looked like her. I sat down beside her and asked politely, are you my fiancée? Instead of answering yes or no, she just ran off. Perhaps she didn't know the answer either. The right time for her to know it hadn't come yet. But if she had just said one word to me I would have known if she was the one. I hope I'll be able to see her again today. This time I'll be more of a gentleman. I'll show her she has nothing to fear from me. I'll ask her to say just one word. I'll say, words aren't important, I only want to hear your voice, to inhale its fragrance. Voices don't just contain the smell of the past, but of the future too. Am I the only one in this city who knows that? When I hear her voice, when I find my fiancée I mean, I'm going to forgive everyone. I'm going to forgive everyone who's done me wrong. Do you know who those people are? I think Serka asks everyone he sits next to that question. He stops and waits for me to reply. I shake my head. In that case, listen, he says. He reels off the names of all the people who have done him wrong. He articulates each name carefully, as though he wants me to memorize it. He stops when he gets to the end of the list. He scrutinizes all the women who walk past us. He is searching for a familiar face. He turns to me and starts listing the same names all over again. This time with exonerating adjectives. Uneducated, he says, ingenuous, poor, orphaned, he says. Faded leaves. The footsteps of the ants that have crawled up my fingers. No one in the park turns to look at us. Under each tree there is a separate island. Everyone is marooned on their own one. This is the shore where life has washed me up. I'm sitting on a bench with a man I've never met before. I accept his loneliness along with my own. I'm so lonely that if someone called my name I wouldn't turn and look, I wouldn't believe it was my name. Why would anyone call out to me? I am trying to find a life for myself. I want to find my past with the same perseverance as the ants, who crawl up from the grass to the metal bench legs and from there to my wrist, I want to find it by myself, in the silence. When people have a past they don't give it much thought, it's only once they lose it that they can't get it out of their minds. But I needn't despair, apparently. That's the doctor's advice. Morning, noon, and night I tell myself comforting lies. In each lie I search for a shred of truth. I study my perceptions as well as my mind. I go wherever my feet carry me. I wander the streets. I sit in the park. Suddenly a piercing scream rips the air. Somewhere in the middle of the park, a teenage boy has snatched a woman's handbag and is running off with it. Everyone is shouting at one another. One of the people chasing the boy crashes into a stroller. The stroller topples over and the baby inside falls to the ground. The baby's mother screams. Half of the people running give up the chase and rush over to the baby. The people dozing under the trees sit up. People wondering what's going on stand on tiptoe and peer into the distance. We stand up too. Serka walks off without so much as a goodbye. He heads towards the baby on the ground. I go in the opposite direction. I slip away from the commotion of the crowd. I leave the park through the small gate. I weave my way through the unmoving traffic and go into the shopping center across the road.

The doors open and close automatically. I walk into a large square. Is this another city inside the city? Every corridor in the shopping center leads to this square; this is where people meet and separate to go about their business. As each corridor stretches ahead it becomes a street, winding and disappearing into the distance. If I ever came here before I'm certain I would have gazed at it with the same wonder. It's nothing like the Istanbul outside. It's cool. Tranquil. My footsteps flow across the marble floor like water. I can't feel the presence of a shadow behind me. It's as though everyone here is shadowless. They only need themselves. Like me. If they occasionally suffer from headaches or insomnia, medicine runs to the rescue. There's a pharmacy on every corner. Not just during the day, there's one for every night as well. All the boutiques, shoe shops, restaurants, cafés, supermarkets, bookshops, locksmiths, banks, cinemas, and children's play areas on all four corners of the city are concentrated here. With its towering walls and endless floors, this isn't a shopping center but a new castle. Widescreen televisions. The aroma of coffee. The sensation of hunger. I try to understand why I left the park and came here. There are no ants. There's no traffic. There's no sound of police sirens. Cameras survey the corridors on all sides. Children run up and down in all directions. I sit on a bench beside a tree. The trees and benches remind me of the park. I observe the heavy shuffle of old people. I examine their faces in case any of them can bring back my past. Don't worry, the doctor said, your past will come back to you sooner or later. I think my doctor watches too many television dramas, she loves talking in terse phrases. Apparently my past won't come back to me when I'm expecting it, but when I'm not. Nothing that I've been thinking about for the past few minutes, nothing that's been going through my mind, belongs to me. My head is full of the doctor's words. I don't know how much of my mind is really mine. The best thing to do is walk. Here I can walk without bumping into anyone. I stop in front of a shop window and stare at the lifeless mannequins. I walk to the adjacent shop window and gaze at a large aquarium. I'm like the fish. That swim in the same place and wander within the same limits. I'm afraid of the sea, but I like the aquarium and the fish. If I live long enough I'll be able to see the days that lie ahead: In the future they'll build a maternity ward at one end of the shopping center and a cemetery at the other. Here people are born, they live and, eventually, they die. Perhaps my other life is like that too, assuming I have another life. The sun here doesn't burn anyone, the snow doesn't make anyone shiver. The sky is a part of this world. As I am going up the escalator I raise my head and look up. Daylight pours through the skylight. The magnificence of large, domed mosques and gothic churches. A tinkling sound chimes from a Buddhist temple above. I look at the people walking by me. Their faces are serene. They all wear the same expression of spiritual tranquility. I wander backwards and forwards aimlessly. I watch a clown act in a children's play area. I listen to the songs. I notice Serka in the audience. He is looking around him with great interest. He's either seeking his fiancée, or someone new to strike up a conversation with. As I look at him, I realize there are so many afflictions that people can be cursed with. Given the choice, would I rather stick with my own troubles, or would I prefer to swap places with Serka? I couldn't say. I walk away before he can spot me. Once again I find myself in front of the aquarium. For a moment I imagine the world is comprised of this shopping center. There's no such place as outside. The shop windows flow by endlessly like a river, and I fantasize about being a part of the aquarium. Glass within glass. Water within water. By myself, in the same place.

## 9

The grocer exits the shop and places a stool outside the entrance. Before he sits down, he checks both sides of the sidewalk to see if he knows any of the passersby. He knows me. I bury myself in the crowd at the bus stop so he won't see me. I don't want him to pounce on me today as well. Yesterday morning on my way out of the house he stopped me, asked how I was, and then told me a story. Did I also use to stop people and make them listen to ridiculous stories? In the grocer's tale two men, one young and one old, were walking on a plain. On the riverbank they met an old woman looking for a shallow stretch of water that would allow her to cross to the other side. The young man came to her rescue by carrying her to the other side of the river on his back. The old man disapproved. Our customs state that touching a woman is forbidden, he said. For days, every time they stopped to rest the old man repeated the same words, insisting that touching a woman was a sin. In the end the young man couldn't bear it any longer, I carried that woman days ago and then I moved on, he said, why are you still carrying her inside your head? When he had finished his story, the grocer looked at me, hoping for an explanation. He waited for me to comment. How's your daughter, I said, to change the subject, is she doing well at school? I have the same feeling of oppression that assailed me when I was with the grocer yesterday. I don't want him to see me. Two city buses draw up one after the other. Most of the people waiting get on. If one more bus comes I'll be the only one left. I look at the grocer, he's still sitting on his stool. I walk away from the bus stop and head back the way I came. My hands in my pockets, I slouch along the road. You shouldn't always take the same route home. When I reach the intersection, I take a left. Maybe I used to vary my routes in the past as well, and always go home a different way. I walk slowly, to give me a chance to recognize the street I am on. A woman at a window is talking to her daughter, who is playing on the sidewalk. A dog dozing by a wall. A couple of cars parked by the roadside. A street seller peddling something I can't see from this distance. A bookshop across the road with a sign saying "Berke Bookshop" hanging above it. Next to it a barber's with "Magic Snip Barber" written in the window. Both doors are open. Are there any streets this quiet left in Istanbul? I wonder what it's called. Should I go back and look at the sign on the street corner, or should I continue and read the name at the end? It's a long street. The surface is cobbled. Each stone is followed by another, then another. They stretch as far as the eye can see, like sand dunes in the desert. There is no end in sight, nor is there any sign of the evening twilight. I remain in the same place, at the same time of day. The barber comes to the door. He calls out to the girl playing across the road. Come here my love. The woman at the window smiles at the barber. Go on precious, go to daddy. I glance down the street. There are no cars. This is that little girl's moment of bliss. In the midst of a game with no beginning and no end, caressed by her parents' voices, in a street that grows ever longer and replicates itself. The girl lets out a peal of joy. The barber beckons to the street seller up the road. He buys a kilo of apples. He selects one and hands it to his daughter. I could walk up and down this street over and over again and spend my days and nights here. I could memorize this as the only route to my house. Laundry hanging on a line flutters on a balcony. A song floats out of the same floor. Who is singing? Is it Kurt Cobain, Yavuz Çetin, or is that voice mine? The balcony is a long way up. I stop and look to see if anyone will come out. The song isn't on for long. It ends. Its voice dies down. I keep going, counting the cobblestones as I walk. I don't meet anyone. When the other end of the street eventually appears on the horizon, I turn and look back. The barber, the little girl, and the woman at the window have all gone. The first wave of twilight descends. Evening is approaching. The longest day I have ever spent outside by myself is coming to an end. I see a watchseller's shop at the end of the street. Its sign says, "Serene Watches." Today I'm trying to memorize all the signs, to test my tender young memory; I wonder how many of them I'll be able to remember tomorrow. I walk up to the shop's large window. The glittering watches on the shelves all show the same time.

I push the door open and walk inside. The little bell on it chimes. The elderly watchseller, busy with repairs at the back of the shop, looks at me over his shoulder. He removes the loupe from his right eye. Welcome young man, he says. Hello, I say. He walks towards me, tea glass in hand. He smiles. For a moment there I thought you were a tourist, he says, I was expecting you to reply in a foreign language. I used to think our knack for sussing people out at first sight improved with age. But it doesn't. No, it doesn't, I say. I describe the clock I'm looking for. He bends down, pulls out the bottom drawer, and puts it on the counter. Table clocks. They all have alarms, he says. The sound changes depending on the clock. We can try any one you like. This green one is a Vaktaki, it's a good price. It's made in Turkey. If you're looking for a Swiss clock I recommend a HertzZeit. This white one. They come in different colors, I can get them for you from the storeroom. I pick up the white clock and hold it to my ear. There's no sound. Give it to me, says the watchseller, I'll wind it up. A wind-up clock. You wind it up by turning this key at the back. This is what you wanted. You only need to wind it up once every two days. It's quiet, you can hear it if it's near you, but it won't disturb you if you put it on the other side of the room. It's a bit more expensive than the other one, but I'm sure we can come to an arrangement. I'm not worried about the price, I say.

I turn the wound-up clock over in my hands, then I place it on my ear. I don't register how much time passes. The elderly man disappears. He comes back a moment later holding another tea glass. He hands me the fragrant glass of steaming tea. When he sees I still have the clock to my ear he says, I can see you're someone who loves listening to clocks. When I was a child this place belonged to my grandfather. I used to come and watch him and listen to all his clocks one by one. I learned by myself that, just like people, every clock has a different voice. What a perfect invention, my grandfather used to say. He wasn't content with just selling or repairing clocks, he used to subject everyone to all his eccentric ideas too. He used to say that throughout the whole history of humankind there have been a total of three great inventions. One was the clock. Thanks to the clock, we understood the meaning of the present moment instead of just birth and death. The clock had no past and no future. The past and the future stopped you from feeling real life. The clock had taught us that, but we still weren't acclimatized to it, we hadn't adapted our mindset to it. My grandfather, who gave me my first watch, said, don't forget what I told you. Value the moment, the rest isn't yours, don't go wasting your life on what doesn't belong to you. That day I was more interested in my first watch than in my grandfather's words. It was only a very basic watch, but to me it was like a priceless jewel. My grandfather used to say that humankind's other great invention was the mirror. The world outside the mirror was one entity, and the world inside it another. When you put them together they become one. When you first looked at a mirror it was a lock, and when you looked at it again it was a key. And in the face of life, the mirror was the source of both our courage and our fear. People should live their lives knowing that one and two were both the same and different, and never forget that they had discovered that thanks to mirrors. I attributed my grandfather's putting the invention of the lowly mirror on a par with the miracle of the watch to the fact that he had first seen and fallen in love with my grandmother in a mirror-maker's shop. There aren't any of those mirror-makers left in Istanbul anymore. My grandmother used to paint designs on the mirrors and decorate them with borders that looked like frames. Don't let your tea get cold young man. I made it fresh. It was my grandfather who got me into the habit of never being without a glass of tea. If he were here I'm sure he would recommend the white clock to you too. Its quality aside, the sound of this clock is totally unique. I pick up the clock and place it against my ear again. All right, I'll have this one, I say. As the elderly man is wrapping the clock for me I ask, What was the third one, the third great invention your grandfather used to talk about? Oh, that? Let me see, what was it? Oh dear, I can't think of it. That's old age for you, just for a moment, you forget the things you know. Could it be fire, I say, trying to help him remember, or the wheel? No, neither of those. Okay, how about writing? That's impossible, my grandfather didn't like writing. He didn't like writing? That's right, he had a story about it that he used to tell everyone he met. A long time ago, there lived a good philosopher and a good pharaoh. The Philosopher, who knew everything and who strove day and night to discover the things he didn't know, went to see the Pharaoh one day, in a state of great excitement. I have wonderful news, he said, I've invented writing. What's that? asked the Pharaoh. By your leave I will explain, said the Philosopher. We are going to inscribe a different symbol on our tablets to represent each and every one of our words. Others who will know what those symbols mean, will look at the tablets and understand them when we're not here anymore. They'll know what we're saying without hearing our voices. Isn't that amazing? Yes, said the Pharaoh thoughtfully. Then he added, But I'm not sure whether everything that's amazing is a good thing. Your writing will distance people from each other. As long as there are words being passed from one person to another, writing will erect walls between them. I doubt that that's a good thing. My grandfather, who repeated those words as though they were his own, harbored the same doubts as the Pharaoh all his life. That's why writing wasn't an invention that he regarded highly. Do you live around here young man? Come and see me again sometime, I might remember the third invention my grandfather used to talk about. Okay I will, I say. I pay for the clock. Just then, the bell on the door chimes. A child in bare feet appears. He holds out his hand. Come back later, says the watchseller, I have a customer now. The child waits a few seconds, perhaps emboldened by my presence. The watchseller speaks more firmly. Run along son, I have a customer. The child realizes he's not wanted and goes outside. I pick up the packaged clock from the counter and go out after the child. Twilight has descended. The car headlamps are switched on. I look up to the top end of the road. I notice the child I've just seen, in front of a cafeteria, under the light of a sign advertising "Ayşe Abla's Café." He's sitting on the ground, murmuring to himself. I walk up to him and put my hand in my pocket. I drop my loose change in front of the boy. I tell him to wait there. I buy two sandwiches from the café. I give one to him. I keep the other for myself.

After I go into my apartment I lock the door. I walk into the living room and look at the rug in the middle of the room. The intricate patterns go from one end to the other. I get down on my knees and, starting from the edge, begin to grope my way along the rug. Under the bright light of the chandelier I search it from top to bottom. It's antique. A finely crafted, hand-woven rug. On the side closest to the table, I notice a pink stain blended into its faded colors. When I walk over on my knees and peer at it up close, I realize it's a bloodstain. Did that blood drip from my foot when I cut it on the glass the other day, or is it a relic of a lost day from my old life? Questions I will never be able to answer again. As I confuse even the names on the signs I saw this morning, I am resigned to never discovering where the bloodstain on the rug came from. Holding it from the bloodstained end, I lift up the rug. I look underneath. I think of evidence of the existence of an old shelter, the remains of a corpse, or, at the very least, ropes used for trussing up victims. Folding up the whole rug, I drag it to one side. Smoldering with a rage I can't explain, I inspect the wooden floorboards. My fingertips move from one floorboard to another. To be certain, I occasionally go back and examine the same place a second time. When I have finished in the living room, I move on to the other rooms. All the lights are on. Starting with the bedroom, I turn the whole house upside down. I can't find anything except dust between the floorboards and behind the wardrobes and armchairs. I am sweating profusely. I think it is only now that my longest day has ended. I can have something to eat, take my medicine, and go to bed. I can place my new clock at my bedside and go to sleep to the sound of its ticking. As I close my eyes, the clock's voice will crawl down to the bedside table like an ant. The many-legged ant, that's white moreover, paces up and down the bedside table, from end to end. It slips into my ear and slowly advances towards the folds of my brain. The determined, white ant. It gnaws at me and causes me pain, but its sharp teeth also clear the blocked arteries in my brain. It has faith in the long night. As the night progresses, and as the ant ticks and turns inside my brain, my exhaustion is unleashed. But still I can't sleep. Who can sleep through the rising and falling racket in the street? When the noise grows louder I get up and look out the window. A group of children are gathered by the piles of rubbish, they're playing in a circle. The tall boy standing in the center is holding a cat by the tail and swinging it from left to right. The other children are whirling around the cat as though it's a totem, having a wonderful time. One of the children is the barefoot child I met in the watchseller's. He too is laughing loudly, and from time to time he prods the cat. The cat shows no signs of life. I look at the windows in the opposite buildings. Nobody comes to peer out of the curtains. Nobody is interested in the noise, the children, or the cat. Perhaps they're listening to their new clocks, or looking under their rugs, moving their armchairs and wardrobes and searching for some unknown object. They don't know that they'll never find what they're looking for. One life at home, another life outside. The children in the street are having a ball. At the end of the game, once they've had their fun, they toss the cat onto the pile of rubbish. They walk away without so much as turning and giving it one last look. The night is just beginning for them. Linking arms, they melt into the darkness. The cat they have just flung onto the heap slowly slides down a bag of garbage. Its emaciated body drops down beside the adjacent wall and lies there, motionless. As it slid, its body seemed to twitch for an instant, or maybe I just imagined it did.

# Its Walls
# Are Made
# of Bricks,
# Its Roof
# of Dreams

## 10

The night, that squeezes into the net curtain in the bedroom, vibrates slowly when the medicines prove ineffective, turning into a bottomless, restless, pitch-covered pit of torment. This night isn't clear like other nights. If Boratin surrenders to the thought he has been striving to banish for hours and takes a few more sleeping pills and painkillers, he will be embarking on another suicide. But it's better first to live and find out what it is that can induce someone to turn their back on life, and then to commit suicide again, if need be. Tonight the ceiling is lower than usual. The room is stuffy. He throws off the quilt onto the floor. He stretches out his arms and legs and spreads his body, drapelike, across the bed. Which day of the week was it? Or rather, which night was it? With the darkness, as sticky as melted sugar, shrouding everything, slithering to the walls, the curtain, even to the sheet, there is no visible crack he can escape through. Yet another night lost in defeat. If outside there is still such a thing as the street, where beggars, whores, and thieves roam, in here there is a disillusionment beyond anything that any of them can comprehend. He has a throbbing headache, in addition to insomnia. Given that he can't take any more medication, he can try one of the books he's been attempting to read for the past few days but has never managed more than one page of. He can settle down on the sofa, take several deep breaths, and open it. It's not the stories that wear him out, it's the letters, the commas, the sentence endings, and the beginnings of lines. Odd looking *g*s that spring up all over the place, capital *F*s, semicolons throw his mind into a whirl. As he links sentences, words pile on top of one another, and the debris builds up. But still he reads on. It takes him an hour to get through a page. One second per letter. He advances millimeter by millimeter. He stops at the end of the second page. He stares at the walls. Just as he now lies in bed staring at the ceiling, his eyes red. Gazing into space. There used to be another Boratin that everyone keeps talking about. That Boratin didn't understand the world by looking, but by listening. He spoke with songs and thought with songs. Where was he, where did that blues singer that everyone praises so warmly go? He made sense of the world's chaos with his voice. He composed music, wrote lyrics, sang songs. He coupled each smell with a voice, each color with a tune. He wasn't interested in knowing, but in feeling. Like the enslaved Africans who carry the dust from slave plantations in their veins and the pain in their memories, he too carried the voice of the new world in his heart. Wherever it was that that man had gone, he wasn't coming back.

He feels nauseous. A wave of heat shoots from his stomach up his windpipe. He places a hand on his chest and rubs it. Now there is only nausea in the place where his voice once sprang when he was singing. Perhaps his blues songs weren't about Istanbul and the world, but just about him. With every tune he shaped himself, sculpted his own marble soul. Then, one night in the dark, the hammer in his soul slipped. The marble cracked. The crack that began in an invisible part of his head ran all the way down to his rib. Every song he knew seeped out of that crack and disappeared. All that remained was an odor rising from his stomach to his nasal cavity. He is going to be sick. He can't hold on any longer. He rushes to the bathroom opposite his bedroom. He leans over the sink. He waits. His hands clutch the sides. He looks at the drops of water out of the corner of his eye. At the rust color in the grooves. At the streaks of dirt. He gets a whiff of the smell rising from the plughole. It's the same smell as the one in his stomach. He retches. Nothing comes out. His fingers loosen their grip. He spits out the acrid taste in his mouth and straightens up. He takes off his pajama top. He touches his bare stomach. He examines his body, as though he'll be able to see the nausea from the outside. He undresses completely. He walks a couple of paces on the cool concrete and steps into the shower. He leaves the large door of the shower cubicle open. He closes his eyes as the warm water runs down his back to his calves. He realizes how tired he is. He feels as though he could fall asleep right there. When he opens his eyes some time later his gaze remains fixed on the opposite wall. He spies his naked body in the full-length mirror. He stares at it as though he has encountered a stranger. He sticks his head out of the water to get a better view. Arms that grow longer in the mirror. Taut legs. Hands that don't know what to do. And a face. If he called out, it would hear, if he spoke, it would answer. It's not clear where it came from, or how it got into the mirror. Boratin puts his hands over his ears. He starts to cry, under the powerful rush of the water. At first he tries to contain his tears, but once he sees it's futile he lets them flow. It's all too much for him. It will all be too much tomorrow, and the next day. He crouches down on the ground, terrified of resigning himself to this fact. Sobbing, he pleads with himself. He has no one else to plead with. He wants this torment to end. The face in the mirror! That face is the only thing that can help him. It can restore the balance of his troubled mind. The bathroom is submerged in a haze of steam. The mirror opposite disappears. Boratin wants to stay here forever. Crying is such a strange phenomenon. While his heart is pounding with terror, his body feels relaxed, in a way it has never done before. He knows there's no one inside his body. Boratin is no one. But he also weighs the other possibility: He could also be everyone. If he doesn't subscribe to any specific identity, he can appropriate every identity he wants. Instead of giving him peace of mind, this thought fills him with a new dread. Crying doesn't help either. He starts to vomit. With his hands on the ground, he brings up a yellowish green liquid. His stomach tenses. All he can see is steam. He knows that somewhere in the steam is a mirror and that inside that mirror there's someone crouching on the ground. He picks up the shampoo bottle on the floor and throws it. He hears a soft thud. Like the mirror, the thud is a lie. This house is a lie. The bridge and the sea are lies. The grocer and the watchseller are lying. The doctor and Bek are lying. Who doesn't lie? He thinks of his sister. There are no traces of lies in her voice. Even though he can't see her face, he knows his sister's voice. He believes in its flawlessness. If he called her now, at this time of night, he would still believe in her.

He waits for his sobs to subside. He steps out of the shower and wraps a towel around himself. He strides into the living room. He picks up the address book on the coffee table. The water from his fingers soaks through the pages. He leafs through them. He's hoping to come across a familiar name. He recalls hoping for the same thing on many occasions, and shutting the address book with a feeling of dejection each time. He shuts it again. He glances through the numbers on the back cover. He stops when he gets to a number written in a large hand. There is no name in front of it. Bek told him that it's his sister's number. He picks up the phone and dials it. Each number passes through the telephone to the cable, travels down through the walls to the damp underground, and, carving out its own path among thousands of other numbers, reaches the telephone at the other end. The phone rings. Boratin knows what he will say to his sister. He will say, help me. He will say, I'm very ill. He will say, why me? I'll come to see you by the night train Abla. I'll go to Haydarpaşa Station, stand in the ticket queue and tell the man in the ticket office that I want a window seat. When the train departs I'm going to rest my head against the window and let my thoughts drift as I listen to the sound that I might be able to remember from films of the train chugging along the tracks. As the metal wheels turn on the metal tracks, I'll close my eyes and sleep until morning. I'll go home with a longing I don't know the meaning of. *Home:* A word that draws me into itself. Its walls are made of bricks, its roof of dreams. The first letter of home will invite me to come in. Its second letter will take me through a corridor hung with faded photographs. Then it will take me into a dimly lit room and put me to bed between freshly laundered sheets. My sister will be sitting beside that letter. She'll tell me about my childhood. I'll doze off as I listen to her. Just then the telephone will ring. Insistently. A cool breeze in the street. A faded star in the sky. Everyone ties and unties, ties and unties the knot of their own life. No one answers the telephone. Boratin hangs up. It is only then that he realizes tears are still streaming down his cheeks. He waits for his breathing to return to normal. He wipes away his tears with the back of his hand. He cradles the telephone in his lap. With trembling hands, he dials the number again. This time the ringtone sounds hopeful. After the second, then third ring someone picks up at the other end. He hears a woman's sleepy voice. It's not his sister's. It belongs to someone younger. Hello, hello, says the woman on the phone. It's clear from her husky tone that she wants to go back to sleep as soon as possible. Boratin can't think of anything to say. His mind goes blank. It doesn't even occur to him to put the phone down. He tries to work out why he came into the living room and what he's doing here. He looks at himself. He's naked. He has the towel around his waist. The red and black phone is in his lap. The receiver is at his ear. Hello, says the voice on the other end. Hello, who is it? Who am I? I'm Boratin, but there's no point in saying it. Because Boratin is a name that can't answer any questions. It's a word that's hollow inside. Hello, hello, who is it? They call me Boratin, and they show me my ID card so I'll believe it. They think my parents' names on the ID card, my date and place of birth are all I need to know who I am. But I don't want to know who I am, I want to know what I am. They don't tell me that. What am I?

## 11

Theodora's Tavern is on a pedestrian street, sand-
wiched inside a row of restaurants. It's easy to recognize by the tables overrunning the sidewalk and the
large, bustling crowd. At the long table where the young
friends are sitting, Boratin tries to respond to his companions' fussing. Have you tried the hummus Boratin?
It's noisy over there, would you rather sit here Boratin?
How about another ice cube in your *rakı* Boratin? Boratin chooses to follow Bek's example and drink *rakı*
rather than join the end of the table that's drinking
wine. Hayala, who is sitting opposite him, raises her
glass and says, Cheers. The entire table does the same.
The tension in the air is soon dispersed, helped by the
rapidly emptied and filled glasses. Platters of mezes are
passed up and down the table. Boratin tries, on the one
hand, to match his friends' names to their faces and save
them in his memory, and, on the other, to keep track
of Bek's conversation, which keeps jumping from one
subject to another. Beauty is more alluring than kindness, says Bek, pointing at a group of women sitting at
the table opposite them. (They watch the happy young
women drinking.) Which one grabs you, asks Bek, the
kind-looking one sitting in the middle, or the beautiful

one next to her? (The woman in the middle is respected by all the others. They listen to what she says and value her opinion. Whereas the woman on her right stands out because she's beautiful.) Don't tell me beauty doesn't last. Kindness doesn't either. Kindness expects to be repaid with kindness, and besides, kindness is limited. Can we say the same of beauty? (As Bek takes a sip of *rakı* and helps himself to a piece of cheese, they all seize the opportunity to sneak a better look at the woman's eyes, nose, and lips.) Beauty doesn't demand anything in return and neither is it out for what it can get. It's faithful. What you see is what you get. (The woman is wearing a delicate necklace around her bare neck. One of the straps of her dress has slipped off her shoulder. She is holding a glass of wine. The smile that plays on her lips as she listens to the woman beside her makes her look even more beautiful.) I beg the pardon of the women among us, says Bek. (There are four women and six men at the table.) Don't worry Bek, we would never dream of competing with her, says Hayala. She caught our eye and we were all pointing her out to each other way before you were. The only person in this tavern tonight who could have competed with her, if he'd been a girl, is Boratin. (They're treating Boratin like they did in the old days. And he is trying to feel at ease amid their familiarity.) If the balcony above that table collapsed and the women were crushed under it, which one would you feel saddest about? asks Bek. Don't say all of them. I don't want to hear all the usual clichés. You're musicians, you turn language upside down. Come on! (It's obvious that they like being at this table, that they tease and wind each other up as they argue over every subject that enters their heads.) They raise their glasses again. Boratin goes easy, taking only tiny sips. When he got to this street as the sun was setting, he thought he would be upset about not remembering a place that was this lively and busy. But two hours have passed and he doesn't feel upset. He doesn't feel anything.

The friend on his right, whom everyone calls Effendi, says, I'm just nipping out for some cigarettes, do you want to come with me? Boratin turns to Bek, like a child who can't decide what to do. It will do you good, says Bek, it will give you a chance to have a look around. They leave the table. They head towards the end of the street. It's clear that everyone in this street knows them. They nod their heads in response to all the greetings from everyone they pass. Once they turn the corner and reach the main road, they are finally free of all those eyes that know them. The street is heaving. It's full of young people. And brightly lit. Here it's easy to be a part of the young people and the lights. They don't even glance at the liquor stores they pass. They look intent on walking to wherever it is that the street ends. They give the impression of having been up and down that street countless times. Once they have passed the large shop windows, they turn onto a quaint old passage. It's quiet. And cool. They stop in front of a billboard pasted with movie posters. As they examine them, each waits for the other to speak. Effendi breaks the silence. People have one intellectual age and another emotional age, he says. As one develops it's possible that the other may fall behind. For example, the intellectual age of all the people at our table is quite advanced, but their emotions are still adolescent. You were the only one who managed to strike a balance between the two, who was able to demonstrate the perfect harmony that exists between intellectual and emotional ages. Boratin, what happened to you? Alcohol has untied Boratin's tongue. He doesn't hesitate to voice what he's thinking. You're asking me about someone I don't know, he says. You're the one who remembers the person you're asking about, not me. You tell me, what happened to him? Effendi grabs Boratin by the wrist. He squeezes it tightly. He stares at him hard and waits. Don't you remember this either Boratin? he asks. What, I don't understand, what don't I remember? Boratin, you don't remember us coming to this passage about a year ago and standing in front of this billboard and you grabbing me by the wrist like this when I told you I wanted to commit suicide, do you? Boratin looks sheepish. It's the first time it has occurred to him that others too might want to die. You were always lucky, continues Effendi, and your good luck came to the rescue again. Dozens of people jump off the Bosphorus Bridge every year. It's like leaping off a tower and landing on concrete. To this day there have only ever been a couple of people who have escaped death, and even they ended up disabled. But you got let off with just a broken rib and the loss of your memory. There was a knot in your mind that none of us could feel. Instead of by dying, you freed yourself of it by forgetting. I used to envy you Boratin, you were good looking and talented, you were everyone's darling. But those aren't the things I envy anymore, now I envy the loss of your memory. Why are you trying to find your past? Let that knot be, let it lie there buried. They say you mix up the times of things that happened hundreds, thousands of years ago and think some of them happened today. Without going back that far, let me tell you about last year. One night after we'd had a few drinks at Theodora's Tavern, you and I left and came here. I was quite tipsy. I gazed at the posters on here and poured my heart out to you. I told you I was planning on committing suicide and that I was on the point of taking the final step. You took me home. You washed my face. You put me to bed. You stayed with me. You didn't leave my bedside for days. You ate your meals with me, you played your guitar with me. It was at that time that you composed one of your best songs. Eventually, death slowly withdrew from me, in the end it was just a word in songs. Whereas before, death used to find me everywhere. On the balcony it used to say, jump. On windy days it would summon me to the sea. Whenever I went into the kitchen it would show me the knife. At night it would wake me up with the smell of the medicines in the cabinet. It was hard to control myself. I told you then why I wanted to commit suicide, this time I'm not going to. As you've forgotten the past, then my reason for wanting to die can stay forgotten too. Thanks to you I pulled myself together. Otherwise I thought I would achieve some sublime goal by dying. Apparently, two thousand years ago, they used to display the corpses of soldiers who committed suicide on crosses, they would drag the bodies of women through the streets with the same ropes they had used to hang themselves. Then times changed, suicide acquired a noble status, it was as though it represented immortality. Particularly among musicians and writers. Because death was tragic, suicide was ranked with greatness. But those times have passed too. There's nothing tragic left in life anymore. Death has lost all meaning and suicide has become farcical. The root of suicide lay in our past, I went to that limit and came back again. Boratin, you have freed yourself of your past, losing your memory has set you free. That's a miracle beyond anyone's reach.... As Effendi goes on with his passionate speech, Boratin takes a step back. He slips his wrist out of Effendi's loosened grip. He realizes it hurts and rubs it with his hand. Are we going to buy those cigarettes? he asks. Effendi pauses. He holds his breath. He hesitates for a moment, then bursts out laughing. His voice echoes in the passage. Of course we are, he says. We can have one on the way back to the tavern. They exit the passage. They blend into the swelling crowd in the street.

They buy cigarettes from the kiosk on the first corner. They light up and walk back to the tavern in silence. They join their friends. Raising their glasses in response to the glasses raised to toast their return, they sip their drinks. Effendi answers Bek when he asks, What have you two been up to? Boratin told me a great story, he says. Did he? Yes. A young man gets lost in the woods. Several days later he meets an old man. The old man has been lost for a long time too and suggests to the young man that they look for the way out together. No, says the young man, I can't waste my time with you, if you knew the way out you'd have found it by now. But, says the old man, I know which roads don't lead out of the wood. That was how the story went, wasn't it Boratin? Boratin stares at him without replying. He takes a large gulp of *rakı*. He turns back to his plate and dips a piece of bread in his meze. When silence descends on the table, Bek raises his glass. Come on, he says, this time let's drink to Boratin's story.

Boratin watches the women at the opposite table. He remembers the beautiful one. (She is telling a story. Her slender fingers are making graceful gestures in the air.) Boratin saw her on Yüksek Kaldırım going into a second-hand book dealer's. She was with a man who looked like her twin, the two of them were identical. The two siblings examined an antique book at the book dealer's. (The woman is a university lecturer. She's telling her friends about an important manuscript that she's teaching in class. Her voice is so animated that it carries all the way over to the eavesdropping Boratin. She is complaining about the students' lack of interest in such an old, rare book. The woman beside her laughs, they're too busy looking at you to pay any attention to the book, she says.) When Boratin saw the woman in the street, it wasn't her beauty that had struck him. He listened to her conversation with her brother and wanted to see the inside of the secondhand book dealer's. (Even now it's not the woman's beauty he recognizes, but the posture of her neck, the slight tilt of her head.) You've wandered off Boratin, says Bek, are you all right? I'm fine, but if I carry on drinking at the same pace as you, I'll soon be bleary-eyed. Aren't you bleary-eyed already, you haven't taken your eyes off that woman for the past few minutes. (The woman rests her elbow on the table and continues to talk.) I know that woman, says Boratin. Bek grins broadly. Beauty can unlock even the mind's padlocks, he says. It's not like that, says Boratin, I saw her on the first day I went out with you, going towards Galata Tower. No, says Bek, I think you know her from before, but you're getting the time mixed up. Didn't you say yourself that you get your times mixed up? Listen to me Bek, I saw that woman going into a secondhand book dealer's. I just eavesdropped, she's telling her friends about the antique books. (Apart from one or two, says the woman, students don't get excited about new discoveries.) Bek laughs. You're drunk, he says. You're drunk more like, replies Boratin. I readily admit I'm drunk, says Bek, you admit it too. No, says Boratin,

I'm starting to feel a bit dizzy, but I'm not drunk yet. In that case, we'd better carry on drinking, says Bek. They take a sip from their drinks. Shoulder to shoulder, they gaze at the woman. Boratin watches the letters and words pouring from her lips. As for Bek, he sees birds with vaporous wings gliding from those pink lips. He sighs. Was she by herself when you saw her before, he asks. No, she was with her twin brother. Her twin, says Bek, you mean you're that certain. . . . I'll just go and find out if it's true, I'll be right back. How are you planning on finding out? Watch, says Bek. Steadying himself with his hands, he stands up. His steps are precarious. He sways over to the women's table. He greets them. The women smile back at him. They pull up a chair and invite him to join them. Bek thanks them. He points out Boratin to the beautiful woman. He says something to her. The beautiful woman looks at Boratin, she remains silent for a while. Then she leans over and whispers in Bek's ear. She turns and looks at Boratin again. With a faint smile on her lips. Bek leaves their table. He returns as unsteadily as he went. He wheezes as he sits down. He closes his eyes. Was I right? asks Boratin. Bek opens his eyes. He stares vacantly. Why don't we have a drink, he says, as though talking to himself. He reaches his hand out towards the table. Boratin pushes the glass in front of him away. That's enough for tonight, you've had too much, I think we should leave, he says. But we've only just started, says Bek. No we haven't, says Boratin. He stands up. He picks up his jacket from behind the chair and puts it over his shoulders. Just then Effendi calls out to the others. Hey folks, he says, one of you take Bek home and I'll take Boratin. Boratin says, There's no need. I can go by myself, it would be better if you took Bek. Are you sure Boratin, will you be all right going by yourself? Yes, I'm fine. One or two people stand up with them, the others look as though they're planning on spending most of the night there. As Boratin is saying goodbye, the jacket on his shoulders slips and falls off. He bends down to pick it up. He feels giddy. One knee stays rooted to the ground. He's too dizzy to stand up. He grabs a chair. Hayala comes and takes his arm. She helps him stand up. Are you all right? she says. Yes, I think so. I'll take you home Boratin, you can't go by yourself.

# 12

Hayala returns from the kitchen carrying two coffee cups. She sits down beside me on the sofa. This will sober you up, she says. I take a sip from the coffee. Thank you. In the tavern I didn't realize I'd had too much. I was listening, watching and eating and drinking the whole time. I thought I would be able to make it home by myself. But then suddenly I felt dizzy. Towards the end you were trying to keep up with Bek, says Hayala. You were knocking them back one after the other, like him. How are you feeling? I feel better now I'm home. I don't feel dizzy anymore. Perhaps it was the crowd that made me dizzy. It's tiring talking to so many people at once. Did I find it tiring in the past as well, looking at each face in turn, connecting faces with voices and then keeping a mental record of each connection? No Boratin, you weren't like that before. You didn't have any complaints about yourself, none that I heard of anyway. Hayala, I can only talk to one person at a time. Any more and it wears me out. The people at that table are my friends, but I found it too intense to mingle with that crowd. The longer I sat there the more desperately I wanted to get up and leave. Maybe that's why I overdid the *rakı* towards the end. I'm used to being at home in the evenings, it felt strange being out for the first time. I feel safe in this living room. I prefer pacing up and down the corridor and going backwards and forwards from the bedroom to the kitchen to being out. Today I left the kitchen in a bit of a mess when I went out. Were you able to find the coffee okay? No problem. Your house is as tidy as it always is Boratin. Anyone who comes here always finds everything in the right place. Who knows for how many generations the armchairs, cupboards, and paintings have sat in exactly the same spot without moving. The boys teased you when you rented this place. They said you're fifty years older than you look. And you replied, I'll have you know, you note-scribblers, that actually I'm not fifty, but a hundred years older. You were into old guitars, old books, old furniture. You probably still are. Your tastes won't have changed just because your memory has. I don't know, Hayala. Sometimes I like this sofa, and sometimes I hate it. I might spend all day lying on it one day, and then not even feel like perching on the end the next. Sometimes I can't take my eyes off that chandelier, and at others its crystals get on my nerves for days. Look at the guitars. They're so beautifully made, every one of them is a work of art. They have soft, curved lines, they're long. There are as many tunes between the guitar magnets and the tuning keys as there are trees in a wood. My mood changes so quickly, the guitars might suddenly seem worthless to me. Who knows, one night I might get it into my head to throw them out onto the rubbish heap in the street. Hayala smiles. If you do decide to throw them out, phone me. I'll take your stuff to my own rubbish heap.

I pick up the address book from the coffee table beside us and hand it to Hayala. Have I got your number? I ask her. Holding her coffee cup in one hand, Hayala puts the address book on her lap, flicks through the pages, and finds her name. Here it is, she says. No one has address books anymore Boratin, everyone puts their numbers on their phone. You only ever see address books like these in old movies. Although I must say, I can't think of anything more fitting for the old phone in this house than an address book with yellowed pages. Hayala, I say, have

I ever treated you badly? Hayala pauses for a moment. She takes a sip of coffee. She hugs the address book to her chest. She looks at me in a way she hasn't looked before. She is either looking at me as a stranger for the first time, or seeing that I've gone back to being my old self. Right now I'm further away from her than ever before, and at the same time closer. She'll either walk out without saying a word, or talk nonstop until morning. Boratin, she says, what's going on in that head of yours, why did you ask me that? I'm scared, I say. I'm scared of voicing what I feel. When my mind drifts into the past I find myself in front of a white wall. It's pointless trying to trace the movements of my life on a stark white wall. There isn't a line, or a shadow. Only blankness. When I gaze at it I realize after a while that actually I am that blankness. Why? I say. Who did I hurt in the past, and how? I think. When my telephone rings, or when I meet someone new, I imagine that person is going to talk to me about all my past wrongs. Perhaps I'm not guilty of any wrongdoing, or maybe everyone has taken pity on me and is waiting for me to recover before reminding me. Hayala places her hand on my arm. Don't be afraid of me Boratin, she says. You've never done me any wrong. Quite the opposite, you've been good to me. Whenever there were any disagreements in the group, you always supported me. Last year I was on the point of leaving and you were the one who persuaded me to stay. When I wasn't able to pay my rent and I owed the landlord several months, you stepped in and helped me out. I don't believe you would ever do anything to hurt anyone. If anyone ever claims that you have, the first thing you should think is that it's not you who's to blame, but them. Hayala removes her hand from my arm. Her gaze still fixed on me, she waits for me to speak. Sometimes, I say, I meet someone's eye in the street. In that brief look I see someone I know. Someone who's angry with me. I'm afraid. When I was meeting all our friends in Theodora's Tavern I searched for that look in every one of them. You were sitting opposite me. Our eyes met a few times. Towards the end, I noticed that unsettling stare on your face too. Boratin, says Hayala, that stare that you say you noticed is full of kind thoughts towards you. People don't just love you, they feel indebted to you. You've touched all of our lives in some way, you've given all of us a part of yourself. That feeling of guilt you have comes from not knowing about your past. You blame yourself for losing your memory. You may be right Hayala, but I can't stop those thoughts from invading my head. Every time I go out, I feel the urge to be kind to people who need help. As if the outside world is waiting for me. That urge comes at the same time as the feeling of fear. And then I think the urge to be kind stems from wanting to redeem myself for all my past wrongs. Hayala takes the cup out of my hand. You've let your coffee get cold, I'll bring you another one, she says. She comes back a moment later with two fresh coffees. Boratin, she says, you used to make outlandish remarks like that about music too, and come out with things that would never occur to anyone else. It's good that you haven't lost the habit. During rehearsals you would stop us in the middle of a song and go into a long explanation of why we needed to change the rhythm of that particular bit. You would talk about the groans of slaves in North America, the curses of beggars in Istanbul, and the elation of young lovers. You would quote from books. You would tell us where the spirit of our music came from and say how it would cry out to the heavens as you beat time. We would put down our instruments and settle in a corner in preparation for what we knew would be a lengthy discourse. It might sound as though all this was ages ago, but actually it was only a few weeks ago. You waxed lyrical for hours on the day you showed us the cover of that Submarine album on the wall there. I look at where Hayala is pointing. At the album covers, at the singers' names. The crystal lights from the chandelier twinkle on the bodies of the guitars. There is a different sound on each string, climbing up the guitars' frets as though going upstairs. I know those sounds are twitching there, even though I can't hear them.

Hayala, I say, I spend hours every day gazing at this wall and these guitars. I browse through my record collection searching for something that will make me feel good. I read the album covers. I try to find something in the lyrics that reaches out to me. I'm looking for the same thing now, as I look at the wall and the records. What's that Boratin, what are you looking for? I don't know, I won't know what I'm looking for until I've found it. Contrary to what everyone thinks, my mind isn't empty, it's overloaded. I'm not just afraid of what's gone from my mind, I'm afraid of what's left in it too. For example, I think about the oldest known fact. I must have read it in a book somewhere; the oldest known form of the universe, of existence, in other words, was in the shape of a small ball. Then there was a big bang and the universe came to be, time began. I want to know about what existed before that. I realize how absurd that is. But then I say to myself, what if it isn't absurd. I don't know what to think. You tell me Hayala, what would you do if you were in my position? Hayala pauses for a few seconds before answering. I would probably take the advice of my friends and family, she says. I would learn to wait and not to fret. Instead of thinking about the past I would dream about the future. What are your dreams Boratin? My dreams? I don't know if I even have any dreams. I think for a moment. Once again a white wall swims before my eyes. A wall going from one end of the horizon to the other stretches ahead of me. One can get used to the dark, it's everywhere, but endless whiteness is hard. Boratin, says Hayala, make a wish, and we'll call it your dream. What do you want to achieve in life? First of all, I say, I want to achieve relaxed, deep, uninterrupted sleep. I want to wake up without a headache. Not being afraid of the past is part of that too. I'm afraid of my past. I have no idea what might come out of it. I'll wake up one morning to find that everything I've lost has come back into my head while I've been asleep. Just like in the old days. I'll find out why I wanted to die. But what if the discovery drives me mad and makes me want to commit suicide again....At the same moment the things I want the most turn into the things I want the least. The things you call dreams join together in fragments and turn into a horrendous fear inside me. Some nights I want to punch the mirror. I stand in front of it and stare at the face there. That face knows me and calls to me to uncover the secrets it hides inside itself. The road that leads from my face to the face in the mirror is so long that I don't dare enter the convoluted, damp passages inside it. In bed I pull the quilt up over my head. I count. From zero to the beginning. Minus forty-one, minus forty-two, minus forty-three. There is no beginning, the numbers are never-ending. What would you do in that situation? Hayala looks at me through hazy eyes. She takes the coffee cup out of my hand and puts it on the floor. She touches my cheek. She leans over and kisses my lips. Her face is half a breath away from mine. Are you afraid of this too? she asks. Yes, I am. Hayala draws back slightly. We've never kissed before, she says. Her hands are trembling. To stop the trembling she raises her hands to her forehead and smoothes her hair. Hayala, I say, I've never kissed anyone. My body is as empty as my mind. In the past there was someone called Boratin, who went out and about and lived his life happily. He caressed women. I have no idea what his life was like. I'm afraid of him and of the things he did. What is this? Hayala draws near again. She enfolds her fingers around my neck, like a bird's wings. Let yourself go, she says, let yourself go to me. She presses her lips against mine.

# You're a Drifter
# All Alone
# in the Street
# of Night

## 13

Bek called in yesterday. He looked in the kitchen. He went to the grocery store and bought a few things. He talked about several films that are showing at the cinema, and about some of my favorite actors and directors. He suggested going out for a walk in the autumn sunshine. I don't want to go to the cinema, or out into the street. I've been at home for a week, I spend the whole day in bed. I toss right, I toss left, I stare at the ceiling, I listen to the muffled conversation coming from the next apartment. I examine my nails, my fingers, the veins on my wrist. I feel there's new blood circulating in my veins. I sweat a lot. I sit up in bed, I throw off the covers. I wipe away the sweat on my neck with my hand. When I look at the light streaming in through the window, I realize it must already be midday again. A voice inside me says, come on. I get out of bed with a gliding motion. I open the balcony door. I inhale the fresh air. The balcony is full of the leaves that the wind has been blowing about for weeks. The metal railings are rusty. Everywhere is covered in dust. No sooner have I stepped onto the faded, withered leaves than I stop. On the left, in the place where the washing line is attached to the wall, I spy a pigeon's nest. I look at the pigeon in its nest made of weeds and twigs. I don't know how I have managed to avoid raising my head and noticing it on the balcony where I go every single day. If I said, perhaps it's only built its nest recently, but then the nest doesn't look particularly recent. The pigeon is sitting on her eggs, observing the sky. She is guarding against the crows and owls hidden in the trees in the street. Or perhaps she's waiting for her mate. When she notices me standing there she bows her head towards me. She thinks I'm a bird of prey. She stirs uneasily. I back away. I close the door. I let her have the balcony to herself. Behind the window, Istanbul once again turns into a static picture. Clusters of clouds are suspended above Beyazıt Tower. The shades of brown in the Süleymaniye district change to gray in the curve of the Golden Horn. The washed-out colors of Balat Hill fade into the mist on the western horizon.

In the bathroom I wash my face and comb my hair. In the kitchen I glance inside the fridge. I place a piece of cheese between two slices of bread. I go to the living room window. I lean on the back of the sofa and eat my sandwich standing up. This side of the apartment looks out onto a different Istanbul panorama. Concrete walls stretch upwards as though intent on cloaking the sky. There are cats and dogs instead of birds. The inevitable pile of rubbish on the pavement reminds me of those old films that defy the passing of years. A woman is sitting on the sidewalk beside the rubbish heap, rocking her baby to sleep on her lap. They are both barefoot. One of the woman's hands is on her baby, the other is outstretched, begging. Her voice is so loud I can hear it from here. Hunger. Disease. War. The rest of her words are in a language I don't understand. The woman must have fled from a war (which war?), and traveled a long way before finally arriving here. Every night she curls up to sleep in a different cranny, every day she cries out on a different sidewalk. She doesn't gaze at the sky, but at the passersby. War begins with lies, continues with lies, and ends with truths. And there are always people left behind. Neighbors. Lovers. Brothers. Sisters. The baby sleeps, oblivious to all of it. Sleeping allows it to forget both its hunger and its mother's grief. Like Jesus who forgot by dying. I turn my head and look at the figurine on the mantelpiece. Jesus is lying on his mother's lap. His shoulders are slumped. His right arm hangs limply onto the cloth beneath him. His face looks partly alive, partly dead, like the child outside. His despairing mother holds out her weary hand as she gazes at her son's closed eyes. She drifts into an endless dream as she contemplates her son's beauty. I can't imagine what that dream might be. I wonder why the landlady didn't take her marble figurine with her. Did she no longer need Mary and Jesus in her old age? Or did contemplating them day in, day out, month in, month out, year in, year out, wear down her faith at the end of her long life? She delivered them into the hands of a stranger, along with all her past. She left, never to return, never to sleep again in the coolness of this apartment. The old woman's faith in them did not lighten Mary and Jesus' suffering. Neither did my lack of faith. What, then, is the point of my having faith or not? What is the point of my having faith or not in my own past?

I remember Hayala saying to me that night, Your apartment is full of figurines and paintings, but why haven't you got any photos? I don't know, I said to her. The next day I had a look in the rooms. She was right. There were no photos of anyone, including myself. No trace of my childhood, nor of any concerts. I walked through the rooms several times. I searched in the cupboards and drawers. At the bottom of a wardrobe, among my winter clothes, I found a photo album. An album that had been put away, out of sight. I turned the pages slowly. Unfamiliar places. Unknown eras. People who laughed in one photo looked grave in others. People liked posing in large groups. There was someone in the group with a childish face who looked like me. But in some photos he didn't. He was subdued. Gloomy. Unreliable photos. Somewhere, in an unfamiliar country, there was a rising moon. In one photograph, a cat was sitting at a window. Beside it, I was embracing a half-naked woman. The woman's face wasn't visible. Her back looked like Hayala's. Perhaps all women's naked backs look like Hayala's. The places in the photos kept changing. I could barely keep up. I shut the album. I held it between my two hands for some time. If in the past I put it away somewhere out of sight, I must have had a good reason for it. I thought that I sometimes needed to trust my old self. I took the album and returned it to the same wardrobe. I replaced the clothes on top of it. I didn't reply to Hayala's message asking if I had found my photographs. I didn't reply to any of the messages she sent me that day. I replied the following day.

Whenever I think of Hayala, my hand automatically goes to the right side of my chest. I can feel Hayala's fingers beneath my hand. As those fingers explore my body, my breath breaks away and floats into the distance. My body is no longer the body I know. I crash into a wave and come to a halt. Hayala, I say, I can't keep up with you, slow down. I can't recognize the sounds pouring out of my throat. I've lost my memory, all I have left is my body, and now I'm afraid of losing that too. Stop, I say, stop. You're hurting me. Lights flash on and off before my eyes. The books I read said the body is the home of the soul. My soul left a long time ago, now that my tragedy has ended and all I have left is a crushed body, Hayala is now plucking that too away from me. I submit to her. I surrender my body. Dim light covers the ceiling. The nocturnal wind flows in through the open window. The whole city and the whole of time gather on my body. Hayala! Am I alive? Yes you are, don't worry, you can't be considered dead just because you're older than me. Am I older? Yes, four years older, I've only just turned twenty-four. What sort of an age is twenty-four, are all ages alike? Probably, I don't know, I've never thought about it. All right, does time always flow at the same pace, did your twenty-four years pass quickly or slowly? Boratin, my time flows at low speed, it passes slowly. And I hope it goes on flowing just as slowly until I go to New York. Are you going to New York, when? Not yet. You haven't asked me, but I have a dream too. In a way, you're the one who put it into my head. Hayala, speak slowly, I'm having trouble understanding you, did I ever go to New York? You went to a lot of places Boratin. One night in the tavern when you were talking to me about the cities you'd visited, you said: People should spend their twenties in New York, their thirties in London, and their forties in Paris. Did I say that? Yes you did, and I believed you. Besides, I want to get away from here. I dream of settling in New York before I'm thirty. What will you do there? The same as I do here. I'll play the guitar, I'll sing. I'll mop the floor in bars if need be, but I'll never come back to this city again. Istanbul holds no promise of anything to anyone anymore. This city has suffocated under the dark cover of its old charm. Hayala, when you go there, you'll be like I am now. You'll have no past. Because you'll leave it on this side of the seas. I'm prepared to do that Boratin. Okay, while I was commenting on other cities, did I say anything about Istanbul, which decade of our lives should we spend here? You didn't mention that Boratin. You could live in Istanbul at any age, you transmit that in your songs, sometimes with melancholy, but also with a strange kind of joy. You create happiness for yourself out of the melancholic joy here. Much as I love our blues, you and our group, I don't think this city is capable of carrying our dream. That's why my mind is always far away. I wish you would come to New York as well. Okay, did I ever consider going back there, did I ever say anything about that? Boratin, you dropped out of university and went abroad, traveling from one continent to another. When the slaves were freed, after not having set foot outside the sugar, rice, and cotton plantations for centuries, they began to roam aimlessly, spreading blues far and wide. You were like them. You even worked on a cargo ship. But when you came back to Istanbul your ideas had changed. You said it wasn't the road we needed to focus on, but time, that that was what our souls needed. You said we should join the past and the future together in the present time. We should be able to vent melancholy, joy, and rage all at the same time. According to you, Istanbul was the best place for that. Hayala, I can understand melancholy and joy, but why rage? You used to say that if we left rage out of our music we wouldn't be able to understand this city and its people, and you convinced us too. From then on you were anchored to Istanbul, you stopped talking about going to New York, or to any other city. All right then, what about Nehirce? You mean where you were born and grew up? Boratin, you talked about Nehirce a lot, but as far as I know, you haven't been there recently. You were working on a song about it. For some reason it took ages, somehow you never managed to finish it. You said you were going to write the song in the classic blues, three-line, twelve-bar structure. When they heard that, the band members all had a dig at you, shouting out the name of their hometowns and commissioning a song about it. But you gave as good as you got. That was last year. You stood in the center of the stage where we rehearsed and said, listen to me you note-scribblers. Hayala, you used that expression before, what does note-scribblers mean? Ah yes, we all grew up studying music. We all rely on notes and solfège. But you didn't know any notes, you said blues wasn't born from notes but from our souls. Did I really not know any notes? Boratin, if even you have your doubts, then maybe our band members are right. They said that you did know notes really, but you thought it jarred with the blues spirit and so you tried to forget all your notes and pretend you didn't know any. You used to laugh off all their jibes. And that day you held out your arms and cried, Listen to me: The west is not the west, note-scribblers, you said, and it's a lie that the east is the east. God is not God, and it's a lie that man is man. Istanbul is not Istanbul, note-scribblers, and it's a lie that Nehirce is Nehirce. You loved getting all dramatic on us.

14

Early one evening, when the city is girdled by the southwestern wind, I go out. I walk along the long, narrow streets. I sit down on a stool in a sidewalk café and have something to eat. I drink tea in a tea garden. I realize how similar some streets look. Footsteps on cracked cobble-stones. Restricted sidewalks, buildings with washed-out plaster. I put my hands in my pockets against the cool weather, and observe the streetlamps. On a corner, where it dawns on me that I'm lost, I ask a man selling chestnuts for directions and buy some chestnuts from him. After a long walk I reach the street full of old buildings that houses The Golden Horn Bar. I see the name "Subma-rine" and a photo of myself on the poster at the entrance. I look at it from a distance. I wait by the wall for the time it takes to smoke a cigarette. It's finished before I know it. I duck my head, go down the side street, and find the staff entrance at the back. I open the small, metal door. There is a dim light at the far end of the dark corridor. The distinctive smell of smoke and damp. There is no one around. I walk up the side staircase to the second floor. I find myself before occupied tables. Everyone is engrossed in conversation. I pull my black beret down over my fore-head and adjust my dark glasses. I notice an empty table by the wall, shielded from the light. I hurry over to it. No one pays any attention to me as I weave around the chairs. I'm both one of them and a stranger. Once I am seated, I remove my glasses in the darkness. I look down. There is a big crowd around the stage. The front of the bar is packed. New people replace the ones who have bought drinks and returned to their tables. Shadows glide from one spot to another in the dim haze. They communicate by looking into each others' faces and smiling. The voices coming out of the moving lips all sound the same, half affectionate, half lustful. Hands caress hands, shoulders lean on shoulders. The night is just beginning. Young people with long hair and glasses. They are totally at home, as though they were born here and will eventually die here. Perhaps humankind's third great invention consists of a single question. They learn that question at home or at school, and then spend the rest of their lives trying to forget it. A burning caress, a moist sip. What exists after death, they ask. Does everything end after someone dies, or does a new life begin? The third greatest invention is a question like that one. No one knows the answer. Some people find an answer and believe it, but believing is one thing and knowing is another. What will become of me after I'm dead? The difference between me and the pigeon lies in that question. The pigeon knows what exists and lives within that limit. I think of what doesn't exist, and try to exceed that limit. I get myself into trouble. Even if I go over the limit and see everything, I forget what I've seen once I return to life. I fancy a beer. I want someone who doesn't know me and who's looking for someone to chat with to arrive holding a beer, to sit beside me and share it with me. I want to lean on the wall, and for someone at my side to talk to me. Otherwise everyone will think I'm miserable sitting here all by myself. I'm neither miserable nor happy. I make do with being aware that I exist, like the pigeon.

The stage lights up. First Bek, then Hayala, then the others come on. Who played what? They fiddle with cables and microphones, they sit on high chairs. They wave at some people standing by the bar. The yellow stage light gradually fades out and is replaced by a dim red light. Bek, who is sitting at the drums, looks at the band members and hits his drumsticks together. Hayala starts playing her guitar. She's wearing a short skirt today. And a hairband on her forehead. She slides her guitar pick over the strings as she plays the soft beat of the introduction. She sways gently. In the place where I stood and raised my hand when I got all dramatic on my friends. Did the world look different from up there? Given that I laughed and joked with them, I must have been happy with my friends. I believed in them. I devoted my whole life to them. Up to what point? Perhaps there was a question eating away at me and I couldn't get it out of my head. I would go to the limit and kill myself. Perhaps I didn't know what I was looking for either. I was removing the distance between life and death. There was nothing else for it but to save my mind from whatever had snatched it away. Now I am sitting in The Golden Horn Bar as someone else. I observe the stage from a table out of the light. Hayala takes two steps towards the microphone and starts singing: *You're a drifter all alone in the street of night / You cried as you were born / No one asked you 'bout being born / You're a drifter all alone in the street of night / You were wrong 'bout people / No one asked you 'bout people / You're a drifter all alone in the street of night / You got hungry, you got homeless / No one asked you 'bout hunger, 'bout homelessness / You're a drifter all alone in the street of night / If they'd asked ya you wouldn't've been born into this world / If they'd asked ya you wouldn't've been born into this world / You're a drifter all alone in the street of night / You're a drifter all alone in the street of night.*

Hayala's voice grows darker, like the night in the song. The song starts off well, but then the fast shift in certain lines causes slight cracks. It ruins the rhythm. Hayala's voice isn't powerful enough to camouflage the crack. With a bit of work the song could flow smoothly. The shifts could slow down to reflect the footsteps of someone roaming the streets alone at night. That way Hayala's voice would flow more smoothly too. Is this one of Hayala's songs, or did I sing it? I take a packet of cigarettes out of my pocket. I light up and lean back. I consider the difference between listening to a song and singing it. I capture every reverberation on the stage, I listen to each individual instrument. I notice that Effendi, who is on the keyboards on the left, is looking at me. As his fingers wander over the keys, his head is turned towards where I'm sitting. He stares, as though he can see me in the shadows. His expression is one of curiosity and disbelief. He gazes unblinkingly. How did he manage to see me at that table tucked away out of sight on the top floor? Perhaps the match I struck lit up my face. His fingers continue to wander over the keys as he watches me. He knows exactly where they are in the song. Just like he knows exactly where I am. What does he want from me? I'm not the man he used to have in his life. He doesn't understand that. He wants me to chat with him, to spend my sleepless nights with him. To pour my heart out to him. To embrace his friendship. And, once I find my old identity again, to feel beholden to him. Like he feels beholden to me. He thinks of that as kindness. He doesn't realize that when he sometimes asks Bek to say hello to me, it's not peace he's sending me, but anxiety. I am not the me who reconciled him with life. And he doesn't hold the key that will undo my locks (so who does hold it?). I look away. I bow my head and lean against the wall. I put my glasses back on. I pull my beret down over my forehead. I take a deep drag on my cigarette and blow out the smoke. I draw a veil of smoke over my face. Enclosed in the smoke, I'm like a ship drifting in an unknown corner of the ocean, shrouded by the mist. No one can find me. The world orbits around itself, just as I orbit around myself. One day when the end of time comes, I will blend into the night, swallowed up in the droning that we are all a part of, and vanish. Nobody remembers anyone. I don't remember. Where is the harm in that? That's what all the lyrics and melodies of songs are about. Hayala goes back to the microphone. She goes on with the song: *You're a drifter all alone in the street of night / You loved like crazy / No one asked you 'bout loving / You're a drifter all alone in the street of night / You got a rose, you got a heart / No one asked you 'bout the rose, 'bout the heart / You're a drifter all alone in the street of night / As you were dying slowly you cried / No one asked you 'bout dying / You're a drifter all alone in the street of night / If they'd asked ya' you wouldn't've died in this world / If they'd asked ya' you wouldn't've died in this world / You're a drifter all alone in the street of night / You're a drifter all alone in the street of night.*

Hayala lifts the guitar neck and touches the strings one last time. She ends the song on a subdued note. She waits in the spotlight. There are raised bottles and glasses amid cries of bravo. Hayala nods her head to the crowd. She makes everyone feel that although the song has ended there are still people drifting all alone in the street of night. Good evening my friends, she says. Here we are, back together again after the holidays. Some of us aren't with us today because they're taking extra holiday. Boratin's not here, but don't worry, before you know it he'll be the one talking to you at this mike. Thank you for your hearty applause, we'll pass it on to him. We started the evening with one of Boratin's songs, and we'll continue with another song he wrote. Hayala takes a step back from the microphone and clutches the guitar neck again. She rocks on her right foot. She sways back and forth. Boratin switches off. He puts his head in his hands. Why, he keeps repeating to himself. He wants to know why he composed the song like that. He's not surprised about the song being his, but about why he left those small flaws in such a beautiful song. He puts his hands over his ears. He doesn't want to hear any more. Just now while he was listening to the song, he had pictured himself beside Hayala and Bek. He had almost believed that he could play with them, that he would be able to go back on stage one day. He had felt bold. Now he feels disheartened, he is losing his will. He doesn't want to watch them anymore. He decides that he won't, after all, spend the whole evening here and then go backstage to see his friends. He remains on the second floor of the bar, like a corpse hanging on a hook. If he listens to his mind, hanging on a hook like a corpse is bad. If he listens to his heart, as long as he is breathing he doesn't care about anything. Which of them should he believe, his mind or his heart? He can't find the happiness that the young people around him are feeling and that music once used to give him. If he is going to find that happiness here one night, then this is not that night. Boratin stands up. He steps out of the shadows and stands in the full glare of the light. He takes one last look at Effendi. He senses him as distant as a faded star, but as close as a shooting star flying towards him. He raises the collar of his jacket. He bows his head. He glides through the growing crowd like a ghost. He walks quickly down the stairs and goes out through the same door he came in. He slips away from the noise and the smells. In the middle of the street he stops and looks up. The sky has clouded over. The moon has hidden her face. The wind is blowing. The side streets are lined with scraps of paper and leaves.

## 15

As I leave The Golden Horn Bar and retrace my steps along the same streets, I feel as though I have come to a new city. Entering each street from the other end is like looking into a mirror. Buildings face the opposite direction. Lines on shadows grow darker. What is distant grows closer and what is close grows distant. The echo of footsteps on the cobblestones is different. Those who try entering from the opposite end of a street they always enter from the same end pause, just as I do. Some undergo a complete change. A man who returns home from this end empty-handed and long-faced appears from the other end of the street the following day with his arms full of toys and flowers. A girl who has quarreled with her lover here turns up at the other end of the street the next day, smiling and reconciled. The wind is blowing hard, lashing at my back. There's no one waiting for me, I'm in no hurry to get anywhere. I walk from one street to another, at a leisurely pace. I stop at the yellow traffic light on a street corner. Everywhere is deserted. Not a car or a pedestrian in sight. The yellow light is on for me. I wait. The traffic light stays stuck at yellow, like the stopped clock in the clock tower. I have no idea how long I'll have to wait. Is the yellow light merely the forerunner of the green or red light, or does it shine in its own right? It's suspended between continuing and stopping, existence and nonexistence. It detains me on the deserted side of the city, all alone in the middle of the night. I can't say how long I remain standing at that crossroads where the winds intersect. Time works slowly during the night. A middle-aged man walks past me, equally slowly. Once he has staggered drunkenly to the other side of the street, he stops and stares at me. He thinks I'm out of my mind. He shakes his head sadly and keeps going. I cross over too. Plunging into the dimly lit streets, I walk close to the walls, trying to shield myself from the wind's whip. I hear noises coming from behind drawn curtains. A woman singing, the howl of a wolf, a horse's hooves beating the ground. The sound of televisions being turned up and down.

I arrive at a square. I look all around me. I ask a street peddler selling chicken and rice for directions to Beyoğlu. Pointing to the street on the left, he says, I take it you're a stranger here, and asks where I'm from. I tell him I'm no stranger, I'm from Istanbul. I buy a portion of chicken and rice and eat it standing up. The peddler's wavy hair and handlebar mustache give him the self-assured air of someone who emerged from the sea two thousand years ago and from the steppe a thousand years ago, and has never left this square since. He casts his old shadow, that even he doesn't heed, on the new era. I know a lot about people, he says, you're not from here, I can tell by the way you keep gazing around you.

I repeat that I'm no stranger to Istanbul, that I just took the wrong road and got lost. People don't have the same perception of direction at night as they do during the day. A voice inside me says I should stick to main roads at night. Even if I get lost on a main road I'll still know the way home. That becomes even clearer to me once I get to Beyoğlu. The illuminated crowd carries me off, sweeping me from one wave to the next, dragging me to back streets, then bringing me back and depositing me at the main road again. All streets have a bit of the texture of a main road in them. People too are all alike. Predatory eyes scan the area. Everyone stands at the ready, equally intent on either hunting for or becoming prey. They live the night as though it were day. They grow drunk on light. Even when they sneak into dark crannies to make love, they carry a little shred of light in their sweat. I feel dizzy. I lean against an abandoned telephone booth with shattered glass. Surrounded by the stench of stale urine, I wait for my dizziness to pass. I examine the flyers on the wall. Song lyrics, ads for concerts, and the names of soccer teams printed in black and white. I make out the picture of the last Ottoman sultan on torn posters. His face has been sprayed with the anarchists' *A*. I know what the capital *A* inside a circle means, but I don't know what posters of the sultan from a bygone era are doing pasted all along the street. I need to get away from the smell of urine and sit down and rest for a while. All the outside tables of the cafés are taken. I walk slowly, in the hope of finding a free table. A group of young people sitting at a table smile at me and say, Hello. Hello, I say. Boratin Bey, they say, we saw you perform a few months ago, will you join us? There are five of them. Two men and three women. They look a few years younger than me. I sit with them. Instead of drinking beer, like they do, I order mineral water. I'm giving my liver a rest today, I say. I ask what they do. They're at university. They come here on weekends. They're into music and cinema. All three women have a pendant of the letter *A* I saw on the anarchists' posters around their necks. I don't have anything around my neck. I don't wear rings. I didn't notice any jewelry among my possessions at home. I don't even wear a watch. If I did have a pendant I'd probably choose the letter *B*. *B* for blues. I'd leave my top two buttons undone so everyone could see it. I'd wear it on stage. I'd wear it to bed. I'd put my hand on my chest in the dark and trace the curves of the *B* with my fingers. Then one night I'd take off the pendant, hold it tightly in the palm of my hand, and leap into the waters of the Bosphorus. I'd consign the *B* to the seabed, among the cold seaweed. When I rose back up to the surface I wouldn't remember what I had left there. The *B* would be no different from other letters. All the letters would become the same. Silently. What is that *A* on those posters, I ask. I mean, why is it sprayed on the face of a sultan who lived a hundred years ago? They burst out laughing. They think I've just made a funny joke. You're right, they say, the man is the head of state now, but he's got the mentality of someone from a hundred years ago. That's why we sprayed his head. Was it you who did that? Yes, during last week's protests. And most of the graffiti in the other streets is ours too. The young friends clink their beers in triumph. I too raise my bottle of mineral water. I realize I've mixed up time again, that this time I mistook a living person for someone from the past. I take another look at the posters on the wall. I try to work out whether politicians bring the past to the present day, or whether they take the present back to the past. I wonder why they have to resort to violence and lies to do that. If they just let people get on with their little lives in peace then it would never even occur to anyone to step out of the circle of the past. Even if everyone forgot most things, they would still live in the circle of the past. I look at the people wandering in the street. They remember things from a year ago, ten years ago. They don't carry an agonizing void inside their heads. When they become desperate they lie to themselves. They cry, they get angry, they sulk. When they eventually calm down they make peace with themselves. Then they look at me pityingly. Don't look at me in that pitying way, I say. Why would we look at you with pity, they say. Boratin Bey, why did you say that? Damn! I'm saying things I shouldn't. The words in my mind spill out of my mouth. I don't know what I'm doing. I try to wriggle my way out of my gaffe.

What I mean, I say, is that I wasn't here when you were spraying those posters last week, I couldn't help you. So you mustn't blame me. My explanation satisfies my companions. The woman beside me, wearing a blue dress, puts her hand over mine. Boratin Bey, she says, let's meet in this street for the next protest and spray the whole place together, okay? Okay, I say, and add, it's ridiculous for a politician in this day and age to think he's a sultan. Sometimes I think I'm someone else too, but I don't go around telling everyone and making a laughingstock of myself. You're right, says the woman, there are times when we all feel that way. But we don't force other people, we don't lock them up inside our beliefs. Otherwise our dream would become someone else's nightmare. The gentleness in the woman's voice could keep me at this table all night. She could convince me of inconceivable things and give me a new past. It's turned cold, shall we go to a warm bar somewhere and listen to some music? We walk side by side, like old friends, strolling through the streets. We pass shop windows adorned with garters and posters scrawled with writing. We go down a street smelling of vomit and walk through a luminous door. We sit down at a table. The waiter heads straight for me. Welcome Boratin Bey, he says, it's so good to see you here. What will you drink? We order beer and mineral water. We glance around at the other tables. We listen to the rock song that the band on stage is playing.

We gradually slip away from the crowd around us and turn back to each other. Despite the noise, we manage to make ourselves heard. We talk about songs and books. If the live music keeps playing we may well make the night, that we began with the letter $A$, last right to the letter $Z$. When we are on our third drink the music ends. My friends look as though they intend to stay till dawn. I feel tired. I thank them for the lovely evening. I stand up. They stand up with me and hug me in turn, as if we have been friends all our lives.

Outside there is a biting frost. It's late at night. I place my hands in my pockets and walk towards the main road. I notice there is a piece of paper in my pocket. I take it out and look at the telephone number the woman in the blue dress gave me. Numbers written in a fine hand, and a name. I throw the piece of paper into the first bin I find. A little further ahead I turn down a side street and head towards home. I drink water from a dilapidated fountain. I count the illuminated windows in the buildings. As I'm turning left at a small mosque, a voice in the darkness startles me. An elderly beggar sitting by a wall asks, Have you got any cigarettes son? You scared me, I say. All I want is one cigarette, he says. He's huddled inside a blanket, at a section of the wall that's shielded from the light. It's as though he's been sitting there for hours waiting for me to walk past. I take the cigarette packet out of my pocket and hand it to him. Keep the packet, I say. The whole packet? he says. Yes, I reply. Are you drunk? he says. No, I reply. Just then the early morning call to prayer rings out. The crows fly into the air. Several shadows coming from the end of the street enter the mosque. I crouch down beside the beggar. I take out my wallet, pull out the first note my fingers touch in the darkness, and give it to him. He doesn't say anything as he takes the money. He waits for the muffled sound of the ezan pouring out of the speakers to finish. Only then does he say, God bless you. I can't speak for God, I say, but I'll be happy with just your blessing. Are you drunk? he repeats. No, I say, you can smell my breath if you like. He smells it. You're right, he says. Does God ever help you? I say. Yes, he replies. In what way? I ask. Well, by sending you for a start, he says. He strokes his beard. I don't have a beard, I say. Sometimes He sends you without a beard and sometimes with, he says, sometimes old and sometimes young, sometimes in the form of a woman and sometimes a man. All right, and who is it who sends you the cruel people, I say. He strokes his beard. That ungrateful wretch who's supposed to be my brother, he says. Why? I ask. Cruelty doesn't need a reason, he says. Would you say I believe in God? I ask. Don't you know if you believe or not? he replies. No I don't, I say. He strokes his beard. It makes no difference if you don't believe, he says, you're a good man. I hope you're right, I say. Do you know what, he says, in the beginning God had something He needed to entrust. He offered it to the hills and the mountains. They hesitated to accept something so weighty, they were afraid. But humans were only too willing to get their hands on it. To tell you the truth, humans were ignorant even way back then, they were evil. They took on a load that was too heavy for them. They lied. They killed. They turned the world into a place of misery. And eventually they forgot what it was that God had entrusted to them. And now we have no idea who carries that forgotten entrusted thing. Maybe it's you.

Before
Finding
That
Word

## 16

It's not clear where the noises are coming from. From outside or from a dream? Boratin keeps his eyes closed. He tries to go back to sleep. When the sounds continue he sits up and gets out of bed. He goes into the living room. He sees Bek looking out the window. Welcome Bek, he says. Boratin, have you finally woken up? Yes, when did you get here? Two hours ago. Why didn't you wake me up? I made so much noise that I figured if you didn't wake up it must mean that you haven't slept in a long time. You're right, I've been sleeping in fits and starts for the past three days, but today I slept really soundly. Pointing at the tea glass he is holding, Bek says, Let me pour you some tea. Okay, and just out of interest, what time is it? Ten. Really, what are you doing here so early? I phoned first, but your mobile was switched off as usual. I phoned your landline, but you didn't hear. So I just got up and came. I opened the door with the key you gave me. Bek breaks off and goes into the kitchen. He comes back holding a glass of tea. He hands it to Boratin. Boratin, I've come to give you some news. Someone you know has died. He was in the hospital for several months being treated for cancer. His funeral is today. Boratin looks at the tea glass in his hand. He knows the ceiling, the chandelier, and his own image are reflected in its water. But he can't see any of them. There's only a rippling shimmer. His dead friend's image may be in the glass too, among the yellow and orange gleam. Who died, was he a relative or a friend? Your childhood friend. You hadn't seen each other in years. You didn't even know that he lived in Istanbul. Your sister told you he was in the hospital. You told me about it. We went to the hospital together. He was so happy to see you. After that you went to see him every week. Oh, then that's terrible news Bek. Why is it terrible Boratin? Well, think about it, I went to see him regularly, it's obvious that it made him happy to remember our shared past. Then all of a sudden the visits stopped, when I lost my memory I mean. Didn't he wonder what was going on, didn't he think I'd turned my back on him? No Boratin, it wasn't like that. I went to see him in your place. I told him you'd gone abroad and that you'd be back once you'd finished what you were working on. Boratin sighs. Bek, he says, you even take care of my absence. You're at the top of the list of what I have to believe in in my new life. Stop exaggerating Boratin, I'm the same old me and you're the same old you. You just don't realize it yet. Bek, you talk to me about my friend but you haven't told me his name. I can't decide whether I want to know it or not. He's someone from the past, I mean he got left behind in the past and disappeared there. He's not here in my present and he won't be in my future either. What do you think I should do? I think you need to know his name. Okay then tell me, what was it? Zafir. Boratin stares into the tea glass in his hand. What can I do for Zafir now? There's nothing you can do. You don't even have to go to his funeral, they think you're abroad. If you go you're bound to meet relatives of his who know you, but you won't be able to recognize anyone. You shouldn't put yourself through that. But I still wanted to come and tell you. I thought if I didn't you might get upset that I hadn't told you at the time, once you found out later on. Boratin takes his first sip of tea. I want to go to the funeral, he says.

When they enter the mosque's courtyard at around noon, they find a large crowd. There are wreaths lined up all the way along the side wall, continuing right to the wall behind the coffin. It's clear from everyone's faces that Zafir was well known and well loved. Some people are crying, others hugging. They are gathered in small groups, talking in low voices, with few words. A middle-aged man approaches them from the direction of the coffin. This is Uncle Ahmet, says Bek, Zafir's uncle. The man comes up to them and embraces Boratin. Boratin is only able to speak once he has extricated himself from his arms. My condolences Uncle Ahmet, he says, I returned this morning and came straight here as soon as I heard the news. My condolences to you too Boratin, I'm glad you came. We're going to take the body to Nehirce after the prayers. It was his last will to be buried there. Will you come with us? Bek intervenes. He embraces the uncle and offers his condolences. Thank God for friends Bek. Just then an elderly couple approaches. The uncle goes and kisses their hands. Seizing the opportunity, Boratin walks into the midst of the crowd and disappears from sight, along with Bek, who is following him. The clouds in the sky cast a very appropriate shadow over the mournful atmosphere of the funeral in the middle of the day. Tall trees are shedding their last leaves. Boratin and Bek walk along the side of the wall and stand where they can see the coffin. There is a smiling picture of Zafir placed in front of it. He is bearded, with close-cropped hair. His hair is greased. He's wearing horn-rimmed glasses. Bek, says Boratin, what did Zafir do? He was a fashion designer. Was he married, did he have any children? He was engaged, they split up quite a while before he fell ill. Who was his fiancée, did I know her? No you didn't. As Boratin fires one question after another he keeps the real question in his head to himself. Why aren't I in this coffin, and why am I the one looking at the coffin from outside, he thinks. He wonders whether the reason everyone in the crowd is so well dressed is out of respect for the deceased or because they're all from the fashion world. What would I be thinking now if I were lying in the coffin and looking at the crowd outside? Would I be grateful to everyone for dressing up in my honor, or would I feel sorry for myself because they were all still alive? I might even feel happy. Lying in the coffin, in a state of tranquility the living can't appreciate, I would spend those last moments amid the voices of the people I loved. I would know perfectly well that their grief would be short-lived. Until my coffin was lowered into the ground, my time and their time would flow at the same pace. Then, when they started to shovel soil onto me, I would leave the time of the living and descend to the time of the dead. I would know they would soon forget me. I wouldn't resent them for it, because I would forget them even sooner. But I would still want to know the answer to the last question in my head: Why aren't I one of the people in the crowd looking at the coffin, instead of the person lying inside it?

The crowd in the courtyard is getting bigger. New wreaths are added to the others lined up against the wall. Journalists photograph the coffin and the distraught faces. At one point Boratin turns around and notices a woman with long hair among a group of women entering the courtyard. He has seen her before, in the café beside the Galata Tower. Throughout the days that followed that incident he thought about her constantly, trying to work out how and where they had met in the past. As usual, it was a waste of time. Boratin heads into the heart of the crowd, saying, Let's try not to be seen. By whom? asks Bek. By the journalists of course Bek, they might recognize us and want to take our pictures too. Come on, let's go and stand by that tree. Boratin puts on his glasses and his beret. It's easier to observe people from behind dark glasses. He tries to understand why everyone looks so tense. Separation must be a hard thing to bear. The dead should be buried and the living should go back out into the street. Everyone should go to their rightful places as soon as possible. That's why they join the line for prayers. They go up to the coffin. They bow their heads before the deceased. Let's leave, says Boratin, let's make our escape while Zafir's uncle is praying. Let's go that way, by the wall. When they reach the courtyard gate Boratin takes one last look at the mass of men crowded around the coffin. Bek, he says, my doctor tells me to be like these people. She advises me to be aware of the past and to lead my life by drawing lessons from it. Apparently that's the secret of a healthy mind. Did you notice the way they were looking at Zafir's photograph just now? They're pleased that that's what he's become. For them, memories consist of photographs. As frightened as I am about losing my memory, I'm now just as frightened of being like these people. I have a doctor's appointment tomorrow but I've decided I'm not going anymore. I'm tired of talking to myself inside my head all the time, and the doctor makes me even more tired. And I've come to hate the word *past*. As I've forgotten the past, I want to forget the word *past* too. I want to cut off all ties with it. Boratin raises his voice without realizing it. Several people standing near them turn and look at him. Calm down, says Bek, calm down, let's talk about it, okay? Okay. Just then Bek's telephone rings. They rush out of the courtyard. Bek walks in front on the narrow sidewalk and Boratin walks behind. At the end of the street they reach a park. Once Bek has hung up, they sit on a bench in the center of it. They look up at the cloudy sky. Rain, says Boratin, when did it last rain? There's a drought this year, says Bek, normally autumn is the rainy season in Istanbul. And once it starts it doesn't let up. Are you curious to know what rain is like? I don't know Bek, I'm sick and tired of everything. And if you ask what is everything, I don't know that either. I stay at home for days on end, wandering from room to room by myself. Then I go out to get some air. The things I see and do during the time that I'm outside fill my head and keep me busy for days. This morning I discovered someone called Zafir. I came to his funeral. I spoke to his uncle. His uncle wanted to drag me all the way to Nehirce. I came across what I thought were familiar faces in the crowd. All of that wears me out. And I spend all the next days thinking, tying meaningless knots between one thing and another. All my sessions with the doctor do is multiply those knots. Boratin, says Bek, don't strain yourself. You need time. I talk to your doctor too, and she gives me advice on what's best for you. She says we have to be patient. Bek, does the doctor drone on to you about patience as well? Yes. Well, in that case let's be patient then. Boratin, there's one other thing. What is it, is it good or bad? Don't worry, it's good news. What is it? That was Suzan on the phone just now. Suzan? Your ex-girlfriend. She phoned from Germany, she's coming to Istanbul next week. She wants to see you. Does she know about me? Yes. They fall silent. They gaze up at the sky's rippling mantle. They see the gleam of a bolt of lightning flashing in the distance. Staring towards it, they wait for it to strike again. Do you think I should meet her? Yes Boratin, it would do you good to see her. Why? Should I see her because it might unlock the door of my memory, or because we might get back together again? What are you thinking Bek, tell me. I'm not thinking anything Boratin, I just think you need to meet.

17

stand in front of the mirror and count. One, two, three, many. In one ancient tribe the people only counted to three, anything after that they called many. To me everything seems too many, I can't even handle myself and my reflection in the mirror. I take the mirror off the wall. I remove it from its nail and place it carefully on the floor. The mirror and I are almost the same height. It's heavy. And dusty. Its silvering has started to flake off. The carvings on its walnut frame have turned black. The carved rose branches are intertwined, climbing along the entire length of the frame. I wonder where to put the mirror. I could put it under the bed, or behind the wardrobe. Somewhere I won't be able to see it. I can be free of it. The mirror's memory has no limit. It draws everything it sees inside itself. It keeps the old me, the naked me, the sleeping me inside it. Even I don't know what I'm like when I'm asleep, but the mirror does. It never sleeps. Perhaps it thinks I'm a mirror too. It waits. What for, I don't know. I too slow down to its time and wait. For days. Weeks. Mornings renew one another, nights follow on from one another. The color of the sky fluctuates between blue and gray. Autumn simply won't pass. Ever since I opened my eyes in the hospital I've been in the same season. I can neither go back to summer nor move on to winter. Sometimes, on moonless dark nights, I can hear the sounds of a miner digging in the mirror. The dull sounds coming from far underground are carving holes in the rocks. It's a mine that's been operating for thousands of years. It smells damp. Every sound that comes from the rocks is the equivalent of a word. Words I used to know the meaning of, but that now seem distant, ring out. I've forgotten my old language along with my past. People speak one language to the outside world and another language to themselves. A language that's kind to itself can be brutal to others. A language that's compassionate to itself can be vicious to others. I opened my eyes in the hospital. I came to an apartment. I saw a handful of people. That's all. I haven't managed to see a language in which I can understand myself. I'm waiting in case I can find it in the mirror. I eat, sit, and sleep in front of the mirror. I wake up and repeat the previous day. I'm suspicious of myself. Because the Boratin in the mirror stares at me suspiciously. What have I done wrong? No one can know what happened before they were born. And I don't know about my previous life either. I'm not even sure if I need to know anymore. I realize that, in fact, a person's life doesn't serve to remember the past, but to forget it, bit by bit. The most distant past is yesterday. Christ was crucified just yesterday. Rome was burnt yesterday. Istanbul was conquered yesterday. That's it. The rest is all forgotten. The mirror alone hasn't forgotten any of it.

I pick up the mirror, place it on the other side of the bed and turn it to face the balcony door. I gaze at the image of Istanbul inside it. The slender Beyazıt Tower tapers up to the sky. The rooftops of Topkapı Palace and the trees in Gülhane Park merge. The Golden Horn, where many-oared galleys anchored a thousand years ago, now abounds with ships with many machines. The mirror doesn't show the last Istanbul fire that wiped out entire neighborhoods of wooden buildings. It does not display the bodies of rebels that are hung from the trees in Gülhane every hundred years. It keeps the past to itself, reflecting only the present. This is enough, it says, this is enough for you. On the opposite balcony, freshly laundered sheets flutter in the autumn wind. Beyond the sheets, a lighthouse flashes in the distance. Stars disappear, then reappear in its beam. I could make do with that. I could get used to this city, and to myself. I could live with a blank memory. That's all. There's just one thing I would want to know: What was there in life that was worth dying for? Why did people kill themselves when death was just a word? People didn't know what death was before they found a word for it. Animals don't know what death is. They don't know what the past is either. They simply live and die. People created the past. They dressed it up with words. On that map known as the past, people were sometimes happy and they sometimes shed blood. The mirror knows that well. It's not for nothing that it reflects Istanbul's buildings and trees, but conceals the past. And that's also the reason for its silence where I'm concerned. The clouds grow denser. The color of the leaves in the mirror fades. There are pieces of broken eggshell in the middle of the balcony. I can't be certain I have seen them. I turn away from the mirror and walk to the balcony. I look at the two broken eggs among the leaves. When did that happen? The white shells of the eggs have shattered into small pieces. They have dried up inside. Dust obscures their color. I pick up a dry leaf. I crumble it into the palm of my hand. Eventually I pluck up the courage to have a look at the nest on the left. I can't see the pigeon there. I step barefoot on the leaves and climb up onto the balcony railings. There are no eggs inside the nest. It's not difficult to work out that the eggs on the ground fell out of the nest, or rather that they were thrown out. Was it the crows who did it, or the seagulls, or the owls that huddle in the rafters of old buildings? If they had done it they wouldn't have let the eggs dry out, they would have eaten them. Did the pigeon do it herself? Maybe chicks were never going to hatch out of those eggs. The pigeon realized that and flung them on the ground. She vacated the nest that she had gone to so much trouble to build and abandoned it. Or maybe she did it for no reason and there was nothing wrong with the eggs. The pigeon was sitting on her eggs as usual. The weary nocturnal cars were passing through the street. The houses were drifting off to sleep one by one. The horn of a cargo ship sounded in the distance. The pigeon perched on the edge of the nest. She examined the eggs at length, as though seeing them for the first time. She turned to face the sky. She waited for a sign from above, for the flutter of wings. It was dark. It was cold. She didn't wait for long. She picked up the eggs, and dropped one, then the other, into empty space. She watched the eggs smash on the concrete. Then she flew away.

I cover the eggs with a handful of leaves. I give the chicks a burial, even though they were never born. I stand up and dust myself off. I go into the bedroom and close the balcony door. I sit on the bed, beside the mirror. I put my hand on the mirror's shoulder. Like a friend. I pick up one of the bottles of pills on the bedside table. I take a pill and wash it down with a big gulp of water. A pill from the other bottle. And one from the third bottle. I'm coming to the end of today. Children have bedtime stories, I have bedtime pills. I prepare myself to sleep. Or at least to try. Perhaps tonight's the night. When I'll sleep and wake up in the morning to find my mind budding with fresh green shoots. When I'll hum the tune of a new composition. I pick up the mirror and carry it back to its old place. I wanted to get rid of it for depriving me of sleep and hiding my past from me, but the mirror isn't to blame. It's not the mirror that's superfluous in this room, it's me. The bed, the curtains, the wardrobe, the bedside table, the lamp, and the mirror are all in harmony. They were here before I arrived. The balcony railings, the opposite balcony, the salty smell of the sea were all here. To be kind to myself I have to be kind to the mirror. It didn't harm me, I harmed myself. Apparently I was a good person in the past, I was happy. Why then did I want to jump off the bridge and die, and become fish food at the bottom of the sea? Become fish food? That probably hadn't occurred to me. Otherwise I would have thought twice about jumping (would I have thought twice?). Holding the mirror on both sides, I replace it on its nail on the wall. I step back and examine myself. The Boratin in the mirror looks calmer. I try speaking to him again. Hello, I say. Hello, he says. I'm a musician, I say. I'm a musician, he says. I'm well, I say. I'm well, he says. We speak at the same time, it's not clear who is mimicking whom. We could play this game every day, one day we might even manage to laugh together. I love you, I say. I love you, he says. I say it again. He says it again. My mind grows weary. There was once a Persian king who knew the names of every one of his soldiers, I'm afraid of being like him one day, of remembering everything. I can make do with little. One, two, three. I can get used to myself, live with little. The rest is too many.

## 18

When I sit in the living room, sometimes everything in it seems superfluous to me. The armchairs, the cupboards, the books I haven't been able to read to the end. If I got rid of some things the apartment would be more spacious. But at other times I think there's something missing in the living room and that I need to buy new things to put in it. I can sense there's something missing, but I don't know what, or what I need to buy. I make imaginary lists. I could buy a television, I say. A vase, a rocking chair, a table lamp. I could take down the album covers and paint the wall a different color. Instead of the album covers I could put up a painting of the old Istanbul, or a photo of my sister. I can picture the old Istanbul in my head, but I can't imagine my sister's face. I haven't got a photo of her. I wonder what she's like. She must look like me. Her voice was like Bessie Smith's, perhaps her face is like hers too. A woman who's a combination of Boratin and Bessie Smith. Does she like music, I wonder. I pick up my address book and find my sister's number. I won't get her mixed up with anyone else again, last week I wrote her name in front of her number. I pull the red and black telephone towards me and put it on my lap. I dial the first digit. The sounds in the receiver pass through the cable tunnels under the city and cross the forests. The numbers glide on the damp soil, like fluorescent insects. Millions of insects underground search for their own path. When my numbers come together at the house at the other end the telephone starts to ring. This time I'm ready. Even if a stranger answers, I'll speak. Instead of answering questions, this time I'll be the one who asks them. Hello...Abla? Boratin....How are you Abla? I'm fine, I'm fine, how are you, I called you a couple of times but you weren't in. I'm fine, I'm working. They said you'd been abroad. Really, who told you? You know it was Zafir's funeral a few days ago, they told me there. They were so happy to see you at the funeral in Istanbul. You and Zafir were such good friends, you spent all your childhood together. That's right Abla, we were always together. Am I lying? That doesn't count as a lie. I can confirm the past, I can consider it as lived. It's as true as the fact that a Greek woman used to live here, that she accumulated furniture, then left it behind and moved out. I heard that from someone else too, and believed it. Why shouldn't I believe what I hear about my own life? Boratin, I hadn't seen Zafir in years. He went to Istanbul and never came back. Did he change a lot? Difficult questions just roll off my sister's tongue. She holds her breath and waits for my reply. What should I say, I don't know? You know, I hadn't seen him in years either. Then, when I went to the hospital, the illness had drained all the color from his face. And when a person is drained of color they don't look like themselves anymore. He pulled himself together a bit, after a couple of visits he sort of went back to being like his old self. I thought the Zafir I knew was coming back. But how much can someone really go back to being their old self again? That too can only be up to a point. If someone's face still looks like their old face, then their smile doesn't, or they use different words. They have crossed a sea, even if they came back they would never be able to find themselves. Abla, who can find their old self in this world? Boratin, look, you're going back to being your old self. You used to speak in that convoluted way when you were a student. You haven't spoken to me like that in ages. Like what? I mean, in that melancholy voice, as if you were reading from a book.... Abla, is my voice melancholy? It's only to be expected darling, why shouldn't you be melancholy? Your childhood friend has just died. But life goes on, don't go destroying yourself over this. Abla, when I saw Zafir again after all those years we talked about the old days, about our childhood. And do you know, I couldn't remember a lot of the things he talked about, and he couldn't remember the things I talked about either. We lived the past together, but we looked back on it from different places and saw different things. And now I wonder Abla, when you and I look back on our past, do we see different things too? Boratin, you're being weird again. Seeing Zafir has taken you back to the old days. Is that what you think Abla? Even if you're right, later on I lost those days as well. What do you mean? I mean that when Zafir died, the childhood that we shared together was lost too. Boratin, that goes on living with you. Look, you're talking about it, that means it's not lost. If you would just come to Nehirce you'd soon remember the things that Zafir talked about.

Abla, I haven't been in such a long time, do you think I'll find it very changed when I do go? Boratin, when you eventually come you may well find it a bit changed after all these years. You'll find me changed too, who knows, you might not even recognize me. My sister laughs heartily. As her laughter echoes in the chandelier I say, no, you haven't changed. You still have the same lovely laugh. Boratin, she says, it looks as though you won't be coming here in the next three years either. Where did you get that idea from? I say. If you were going to come you would have come for Zafir's funeral. Abla, don't think like that. Zafir's death upset me a lot. But rather than grieving with his relatives I preferred to grieve by myself. That's why I didn't go with them. Boratin, you're busy, and you're exhausted, I can tell by your voice. If you want, I can come to Istanbul and stay with you for a few days and look after you. There's no need, I say, I'll be going to see you soon. And this time I'm staying for a long time. I'd love that so much, she says. We'll be waiting here with open arms. These days Aladdin keeps asking about you too. When you come don't go spending a lot of money on presents for him. He'll be happy just to see you. If you just bring us some *pişmaniye* that will be more than enough. *Pişmaniye*? Yes, the one they sell on the train. We can give our elderly neighbors some too, but we'll give most of it to Nana Koki at the end of the garden. She hasn't got any teeth left. But she can eat *pişmaniye*. You know how she's been losing her memory these past years; well, when she lost all her teeth this year her memory went too. She can't remember a thing. Really, I say, so it's got that bad then? Yes, all she does all day long is sing songs in her garden. If the neighbors didn't take her food every day she'd even forget to eat. That's really sad Abla, poor old woman. Do you remember what Nana Koki said to you the last time you were here? What did she say? Boratin, are you turning forgetful too? No Abla, my teeth are all in my head. Silence descends between us. Taking my comment as a joke, my sister waits for me to laugh. Apt liar though I am, I can't manage a laugh. It happens to us all, I say, so obviously I forget things too then. It happens to us all, says my sister. The last time you came, after we buried your brother-in-law, you went to see Nana Koki. When she saw you in the garden she thought you were tending your pigeons, just like in the old days. My son, she said to you, it's cruel to keep those birds cooped up, set them free. And you told her you had emptied your pigeon coop years ago and that you were there to visit her. She didn't really believe you. Set the birds free, she repeated, that bird picture on your back is enough for you. I try to see myself in my sister's words. An adolescent Boratin. A pigeon coop in the garden of an old woman living behind our house. Multicolored pigeons. A tattoo of a pigeon on my back. I remember, I say. That day, that conversation. I liked Nana Koki. And she loved you Boratin. If she saw you now she'd still love you, even though she's lost her memory. Is that possible Abla, can someone who's lost their memory still love someone? Of course. People don't love with their minds but with their hearts. The feelings in your heart aren't going to vanish just because the information in your mind has gone. I want to believe my sister's words. I want to say, I love you Abla. I love you, I say. But do I say it to myself, or does my voice enter the receiver and glide underground like fluorescent insects all the way to her, I can't be certain. Once, said my sister, you were ill in bed with a high temperature. At that time a snake had started going to the pigeon coop. One night Nana Koki kept guard by the coop and killed it. She cried out in the middle of the night and called you to the window. She showed you the snake in the dark. You were afraid. Yes, I say, I'm scared of snakes, even when they're dead, and I'm even more scared in the dark. Abla, I want to ask you about someone. I saw a woman at Zafir's funeral. She's about my age, my height. She's got long black hair down to her shoulders. With long, severe eyebrows. She always has a cigarette in her slender fingers. Does that description ring any bells for you? Is she attractive? I suppose so. What do you mean, I suppose so, either she is or she isn't. Okay, she's attractive. I wonder if it's our Eylül? Eylül? Yes, you and Eylül grew up together. She's blossomed and turned into a real beauty, maybe that's why you didn't recognize her. Don't worry Boratin, I'll find out where she is. It doesn't matter Abla, I suddenly remembered so I thought I'd ask. I'm more concerned about poor Nana Koki. Don't worry about her Boratin, Nana Koki is in a state of bliss now. What do you mean? When she lost her teeth and her mind she returned to a state of innocence, she's like a newborn baby now. She can't be held accountable for her past sins anymore. My sister is more reassuring than the doctor. Her words aren't convoluted. She puts me at ease without burdening me with anything, without wearing down my mind. I run my tongue over my teeth as I listen to my sister. My teeth are fine. They're all in my head. If, when I jumped off the Bosphorus Bridge, I had broken my teeth instead of my rib, I could have left not just my past at the bottom of the sea, but my fears and preoccupations too. Abla, I say, a pigeon came and built a nest on my balcony, maybe it sensed that I used to keep birds. But a few days later it threw its eggs on the floor and abandoned its nest. Bo-ratin, birds can be ill-fated too, just like people. Perhaps its eggs weren't fertilized. She realized she wouldn't get any chicks and flew the nest. She'll come back soon and lay new eggs. Don't touch the nest. You just have to be patient. My sister's talking about patience too. Do they use that word this much in other languages as well? Isn't there another, more powerful word that can be used instead of *patience*, one that's capable of taking someone by the hand and raising them to their feet? You're right Abla, the pigeon will be back, but I hope it returns before the weather gets cold. It's almost winter Boratin, here it's not just cold, it's raining more too. Raining? Yes, why does that surprise you? I'm surprised because in Istanbul it hasn't rained for months, is it raining there right now? Yes, it's pouring. Abla, will you put the telephone by the window so I can hear the sound of the rain. The echo on the telephone enters the tunnel of cables, traverses the cool soil at the roots of the forest, drips strand by strand out of my phone in Istanbul, and pours into my ear. It's different from the sounds I've been hearing all these weeks.

# If I Try Changing One Cog

## 19

The night has a smell of its own. Seaweed muddies the tarmac. Dried branches are coated with dust from building sites. The damp from the walls flows to adjacent neighborhoods. Floating gently, on a wind perfumed with incense, from cellars to lofts, from gardens to under bridges, the smell of the night enfolds the whole of Istanbul. Somewhere in the night lies Hayala's smell. What time is it? The sound of sirens rings out in the distance. There are no other sounds outside. I refill my empty glass with wine. I take a sip. The red wine slides down my throat with an acrid aftertaste. Cheers Boratin, I say. I put the glass down on the table. The surface of the table is checked, like a chess board. Black and white squares. I didn't buy this table, my landlady left it behind, I hope. I consider the other possibility. Just like the flaws in that song I composed are mine, this table could be mine too. I count the squares. Each time I go back to the beginning and start again, as though I'm likely to get a different result. Hoping it will make me feel sleepy. On the black squares I fantasize about being asleep, but on the white squares I realize I'm sitting at the table. I bend down and smell its wood. The smell of varnish blends into the night. Perhaps that smell really exists, or perhaps I'm conjuring it up in my mind. I smell it again. Varnish. Trees. The tree's damp roots wrenched out of the soil. Water flowing to the roots. For some reason the water reminds me of the white clock. I look at it ticking on the mantelpiece. I glanced at it while I was having dinner, it said seven o'clock. When it passed eight, nine, ten, eleven, twelve, and came to one, I don't know. If a thousand years passes like one night, on a wind perfumed with incense, should I sink into despair, or should I let myself go in the stillness of time? Someone who possesses one night can possess a thousand years. Or the reverse. Someone who can't possess one night definitely can't possess a thousand years. The Mary and Jesus beside the clock look as though they too have yielded to time. Their mouths are shut. Their marble faces are as still as a lake. I wind up the clock every night and place it beside them. They wait patiently. For what, I can't work out. I look at the picture of the ant on the clock in the hope that it will help me find the answer. There is a white ant on the clock face. It carries the clock on its back, with every tick it moves its spindly legs back and forth. It goes forwards and at the same time counts on the spot. Day and night it keeps going, but it doesn't get anywhere. I believe white is the best color for time. I pick up the clock and place it beside the wineglass. The night is in no hurry, neither am I. As I sip my wine I could open up the clock and tinker with it for a while. The thought is appealing. I go into the kitchen and return with the tool box. I remove the small screwdriver from the top section. I turn the clock over. I pull out the winding key with my hand. I undo the screws on either side of the cover with the screwdriver. I line up the winding key and the first screws on the squares on the table top. So they will be easy to find when I'm reassembling the clock. I remove the alarm hand too and place it in the next square. When it's the turn for the dial for adjusting the clock, I realize that it only goes forwards. When I turn it backwards it comes loose. I don't bother trying to make sense of that. I place that dial too in a square. I slowly raise the back cover. I'm seeing the inside of a clock for the first time in my life. I wouldn't have seen it in my previous life. I don't know the names of the cogs, coils, and screws that are coming to life in the crystal light of the chandelier. The cogs spin at different speeds, in different directions. I can't see the ant. It has fled inside the clock, to get away from the sudden flood of light. It has gone right to the bottom, to the dark side of time. It hadn't occurred to me that a clock the size of my palm could have so many cogs. Cogs with serrated edges that tessellate with other cogs have created a covered sky, and they rotate. Or rather, the world and the sky rotate around them. The fate of everything depends on them. The sound of the clock, that can barely be heard from a distance, now rings out as loud and clear as a grinding stone. If I fell asleep here, if I rested my head on the table and drifted off, it wouldn't be long before the sound woke me up. Is it the collective sound of all the cogs, or is it the work of a single cog? I examine a medium-sized cog, wondering if that's where the sound is coming from. I glance at the large cog at the bottom. I descend layer by layer, trying to find the source of the sound. I know that when I remove one of those cogs the clock will stop and the sound will cease. Which cog is it? I sip my wine and take a deep breath. On top of the cogs, a rectangular piece of metal with screws on all four corners holds all the pieces together. I undo all four screws. I remove the rectangular piece of metal. I place the screws and the piece of metal on one of the black squares on the table. I must be a bit of a handyman. My fingers are skillful with the screwdriver. Perhaps I repair my own guitars too, doing everything from changing the guitar magnets to adjusting the neck. It's not as difficult as deciphering the cogs in the clock. Time in the cogs both moves forward and goes round and round in the same place. If I could figure out how that's possible I might be able to figure out life too. Why does the pain of a crucifixion from two thousand years ago continue to this day? Why does the throbbing in my rib come from deep down, as though it's the continuation of an old pain? I think of Hayala's words: There's a difference between the past and history. While everyone is trying to give you a past, what they're actually giving you is a history. In the former everything is alive, in the latter it's dead. Yes but how can I tell the two apart? If I asked my doctor she would prescribe new medicines. If I asked Bek, he would look at me with concern. If I asked Hayala she would kiss me. If I asked my sister she would say, I miss you. I miss her too, but I don't know what it is that I miss. I feel sleepy. It's as though someone is dimming the lights. Dark water pours into the empty space in my mind. I rest my head on the table. I close my eyes. Springs, coils, screws. One of the cogs isn't turning properly. I don't know which. If I try changing one cog, they'll all stop.

## 20

You and Suzan used to come to this café, says Bek. After you split up you never set foot here again. Or if you did, I don't know anything about it. The inside is done up like a house, they've made the outside look like a garden. You used to spend a lot of time here. You would read and she would draw. I look around me as I listen to Bek. Despite the age of its buildings, the walls covered with ivy and drawings give the café, which is spread over two buildings facing each other, an air of liveliness. The narrow, pedestrian street really does resemble someone's back garden. The small pots of violets, geraniums, and orchids on the tables are aburst with color. Young people, slumped in low chairs, are chatting lethargically, or reading. Suzan's coming tomorrow, says Bek, this is where you're going to meet. It would have been better if you'd waited till tomorrow and discovered this street with her. I can't understand why you insisted on coming today. I haven't got any memories to share with you about this place, but Suzan has. Are you afraid of meeting her? Without turning to face Bek, my eyes fixed on the drawings on the walls, I say, yes. If you ask me that question again I'll answer, no. I don't just feel one thing, I feel several things all at the same time. I'm both curious and indifferent about my past. I want to come here tomorrow and I don't. I thought I'd come today, to confirm what I want, to test myself here too. Otherwise I can't differentiate between right and wrong. I loved a girl and then we split up. What if I did something terrible to her, what if I find that out tomorrow? I'm afraid of that, but I'm also afraid of not discovering anything tomorrow, of returning home with the same mind, of not knowing myself. So far all my tests have been a waste of time. Guitars and songs haven't brought my memory back. Doctors, grocers, pigeons. Address books, dead friends, black-haired women. None of them has helped me remember the past. My suicide doesn't make any sense. Why did I want to die? Maybe I was one of those people who are secretly unhappy. I was unhappy because I nurtured the wrong dreams. I rack my brains day and night trying to work out what those dreams might have been, but I can't. And then I feel happy. I say I'm free of wrong dreams. Bek, now you're going to get up and leave me, to go to the rehearsal for the weekend's concert. Before you go I want you to know this. I'm not coming here tomorrow. I'm not going to meet my ex-girlfriend. The moment I sat here I became certain of the thought that's been going round and round my head for days. Don't say anything, I think every one of your words contains a secret. I get confused. I struggle day and night to uncover the secret in your words, but always end up in a dark tunnel. I can't do it like this Bek, find me another way. You tried to take me to the past, but it didn't do any good, this time try taking me away from it. Take me somewhere where the past can't reach. You're the only one who can do it. Do you know something Bek, contrary to what you think, I don't long for the past. I don't feel nostalgic about it. I have a pretty good idea of how people live their lives. In the beginning, in their youth, people dream about the future and build utopias. They are hopeful. The future is long and everything is possible there. But towards the end of a lifetime, possibilities are tried out and used up. There's no place left for utopia. People distract themselves with what they have, in other words, with an ample past. And then nostalgia takes over from utopia. I don't have those things. I have neither utopia nor nostalgia. Does that mean I can be considered dead, or am I some kind of solitary living species?

Boratin...Boratin....I turn at the sound of Bek's voice. Are you all right, he says, you drifted off. It's only then that I realize I was talking to myself. I'm fine, I say, I was engrossed in those lovely drawings on the wall. The more I look at them the further away they seem. It's turned cloudy, says Bek, it got dark early, that's why the drawings give you that impression. Are those rain clouds? I ask. I think so, he says, this time it's really going to rain. It's the first time I've seen clouds so close up, I say. If I go up to the rooftop I'll be able to touch them. If it rains I don't know what I have to do, should I stay here, or should I go inside? When it rains wait for a bit, he says, get a feel for what it is and then go inside. Otherwise you'll get drenched. Watching the rain from inside, from the window, is nice too. Do you know something Boratin, you wrote a great song about rain. It can be the opening number at the concert this weekend, we can sing your song. Bek looks at my face and waits for my reaction. There's no point in looking at me, I say, I don't remember the song. I'm sure it's a song with minor defects hidden inside it. Why do you say that Boratin, it would never occur to anyone to pick holes in your songs. If you listened to it now you'd see how mistaken you are. Shall I sing it to you? No, don't, I say, I'll find bits where the lyrics don't fit the music and I'll get into a mood. Bek doesn't understand why I said that. He doesn't insist. I'd better go, he says, or I'll be late for the rehearsal. He stands up. Then he orders a rice pudding from the waiter, who comes up just at that moment. You used to like the rice pudding here, he says, just taste it. He puts his hand on my shoulder. Let's talk tomorrow, he says, tomorrow everything will be all right. I'm going to tell you something, I say. Go ahead, he says. I'm going to go and see my sister, in Nehirce. When are you going, he says. As soon as possible, I say. Bek remains standing for a few seconds, then sits back down again. How soon is as soon as possible? he asks. He imagines what's going through my head. He knows me better than I know myself. Bek, I say, I'm content with what I have left from my old life. You, one or two others, and the guitars that I haven't touched yet. I don't feel like there's anything missing. My ex-girlfriend isn't something that's lacking in my life. The only person from my past I want to reach out to is my sister. She's been waiting for me for weeks, years maybe. Every time, I tell her I'll go and see her soon. What am I waiting for? You tell me, what am I waiting for? Go whenever you like, says Bek, in a soothing tone. You have to start taking your life into your own hands sometime. But do it soon, otherwise you might change your mind. Okay, I say, you go now, you'll be late for the rehearsal. I'll stay a bit longer, we can chat, he says. No, I object, I can't have you keeping the others waiting because of me. All right, he says, but keep your phone switched on. I will,

I say. Otherwise I'll worry, he says. He smiles, his eyes half closed. He stands up again. He smooths back his hair. He looks around him. He picks up his bag and goes. I watch Bek walking, I watch his head bowed with concern, and I watch him disappear at the end of the street. I drain my cup of coffee. I stub my cigarette out in the ashtray. I don't touch the rice pudding the waiter brings. I pay the bill and leave.

I stride quickly through the streets. At each corner, before crossing to the other side, I gaze up at the sky. Fifteen minutes later I arrive home. I pack my rucksack. A few changes of clothing, a couple of records, that's all. The records are for my nephew. I now switch off the lights that I always leave on. I run down the stairs. I put the rucksack down on the edge of the sidewalk. I raise my hand to hail a cab. Our grocer is nowhere to be seen. He must have a customer. Before long a taxi draws up. I say I'm going to Haydarpaşa Train Station. Right away young man, says the driver. He has gray hair and thick glasses. He's wearing a suit and tie. He's very likely a retired civil servant. As he drives into the heavy traffic he says, This is because of the gas tanker. What gas tanker? I say. There's been an accident in the Bosphorus with a gas tanker, all the ferries have been suspended, they've been talking about it on the radio all afternoon. Now everyone's trying to cross over to the other side by car. I hope you're not in a hurry. I still have some time, I say, it's not evening yet. In the back seat, by the window, I look up. I listen to what they're saying on the radio. They're talking about soccer matches. They switch from praise to criticism of the teams, the coaches, the players. I remember every name they mention. That side of my memory is still fresh. I only confuse the time of one player. I assumed he was still alive, but it turns out he's been dead for many years. After that there's a music program. One Arabesk song plays after another. Our car inches its way to the Bosphorus Bridge, amid the deafening horns of irate drivers. The evening's darkness cloaks the horizon. The lights on the other side begin to come on at the same time as the lights on the bridge. The traffic advances at a snail's pace. And then the radio announces that the accident involving the petrol tanker is under control and that the ferries are up and running again. Time for the sea to come back to life. If I could pluck up the courage to look down I'd see the ships sailing on the Bosphorus. I can make out the lights of the boats to-ing and fro-ing like fireflies between Beşiktaş and Üsküdar. If I could distract myself with the ships and the boats' lights I'd be able to stop thinking about the night of my suicide. No matter how hard I try, I don't succeed. It's all reenacted before my eyes, as though I'm watching a film. On the last night of my previous life too I was slumped in the back seat of a taxi, just like now. I was alone. I wanted to sleep. Maybe I was dreaming. When was it, a month ago, two months ago, or two thousand years ago? Eventually I woke up. I saw that the cars were stuck in a traffic jam. My taxi driver was standing outside, talking on the telephone. Other drivers had got out too, and were looking at the accident further ahead. I realized I was in the middle of the Bosphorus Bridge. Instead of the traffic, I thought about the sea. I opened the door of the taxi and went to the edge of the bridge. I gazed at the sky and the lights on the other side. Mustering up all my courage, I climbed onto the metal railings. I held out my arms. I took deep breaths. I waited for the wind that would carry me off. It was night. Perhaps that was why I didn't realize just how deep the sea was. The darkness made me forget about depth. Istanbul was buzzing. The sounds coming from the shores and the slopes all became a single buzz. In the middle of Istanbul, in the middle of the sea, in the middle of the night, between two continents, in the middle of the world and in the middle of life I was as light as a feather. I couldn't hear the shouts of the people around me. I wanted to go back to sleep. I closed my eyes and released myself into the void. Like a bird. That's what the taxi driver said. And as he described it he moved his outstretched arms up and down like wings.

t's completely dark when we arrive at Haydarpaşa Station. I glance around. Except for a couple walking hand in hand on the seafront and another couple sitting on a bench, there's no one around. The jetty farther ahead is deserted. A ferry stands there with its lights switched off. Why is it so quiet, I ask, is it because it's midweek? The taxi driver turns around and looks at me. Have you come here to meet your girlfriend son? he asks. No, I say, I've come to take a train. You're obviously not from here, he says. Where did you get that idea from? I say. Don't you know that the train station's closed and that the trains don't run anymore? he says. Really, I say. I gaze at the station's large, brightly lit facade. If the station's closed, I say, then why are all the lights still on? They illuminate it to make it look pretty from a distance, he says, it attracts tourists, youngsters meet here. When did it close, I say, and why? A few years ago the station roof caught fire, he says, all the trains were suspended. The trains go from the other side of Istanbul now, from Pendik. I'll take you there if you want. No, I say, I'll get out here, I'll have a look around, and admire the Istanbul on the other side. You're not from here, he says, you might as well get a view of Istanbul from this angle too, now that you've come. This time I go along with the taxi driver's assumption. That's right, I'm a stranger here, I say. Have you just arrived? he asks. It's been a few months, I say. I thank him and pay the fare. I get out of the taxi and wave after him, as though seeing off a close friend. He sounds his horn in return.

I put my rucksack down on the first step. I raise my head and gaze at the rows and rows of windows and the station's towers reaching up to the dark sky. I climb up the steps. I come to the great door on the right-hand side of the station. The jambs are made of the kind of dark wood that looks aged as it wears. The door pledges a new world to everyone who passes through it. I push it. It's closed. I try again. It's clearly locked. I peer through one of the windows in the door, looking for signs of life inside. Nothing is visible but darkness. I hold my breath. I'm expecting to hear a locomotive inside, or a whistle, or the crackle of a loudspeaker making an announcement to the passengers. Instead, I hear the deafening shriek of seagulls. I raise my head and look up. A flock of seagulls is flying over me, one after the other. They're so close I can feel the current from their wings in my hair. I notice the large arched window between the station's two doors. Its glass is all different colors. Above it is a clock with a white face. It has stopped. The hour and minute hands may well be positioned at the precise moment when the fire began. They remain motionless, at 3:30. The harsh southwestern wind lashes at the clock. I raise my collar and huddle into my coat. I sit down on the steps, like someone who has nowhere to go. I contemplate the other side of the sea, the opposite shore. The domes, minarets, and towers are illuminated on that side too. The two continents of Istanbul are staring at each other, with the same lights. Everyone who sits on one shore and observes the other side can imagine what they look like from the opposite shore. As though they are gazing into a distant mirror. I too think of someone sitting on the opposite shore, like me, the pain in his rib stabbing harder the colder it gets. I'm worried about him. He can't take the train, he can't go back to his hometown. He doesn't know what to do, apart from sit here. The waves are angry. The clouds are thick and dense, as though intent on wreaking vengeance on the moons. I am alone. Like the empty ferry anchored at the jetty. The doors of the jetty are closed, its lights switched off. Why do they anchor ferries at a jetty that's not used anymore? The lighthouse at the end of the breakwater shines for that ferry, informing distant passing ships of its whereabouts. As I gazed out of the open door of my balcony in my apartment on the opposite shore, I used to see the lighthouse and think the flashing light was summoning me here. Every night, bit by bit, I carved out a path for myself leading here. Of course I knew about the fire at Haydarpaşa Station, but I was under the impression that it had happened a hundred years ago. The lighthouse isn't to blame for that. It guided me to the right place, but didn't mention anything about time. It flashed on and off in the calendar of darkness.

The couple sitting on the bench below get up and leave. It's not long before the couple strolling on the seafront follow suit. A lizard appears under my foot. Who knows where it came from. Perhaps from under the station door that keeps the darkness locked inside it, or perhaps from the deck of the ferry lying at the jetty. The lizard has a slender waist and a long tail. Its green skin slithers across the slippery marble. It stops beside a crevice. It raises its head, sniffs the air, and listens to the wind. Just then my phone beeps. A message. It's not Bek, he prefers to call. My messages are all either adverts, or from Hayala. I open it and read it. How are you doing, writes Hayala, I'm here if you need anything. I know she's there. Although we've only met once, I feel as though I've known her for years. She's understanding about my unresponsiveness to her messages. When I do occasionally reply she says, don't force yourself to write to me. Just don't forget I'm here, that's all. I don't forget. Tonight I was planning to write to her from the train. I was going to say, I'm on the train. I was going to say, I'm off to stay with my sister for a while. I was going to say, the passengers next to me are asleep. The metal wheels slide over the tracks as though they're singing a lullaby. I watch the darkness out of the window. I'm waiting for a song that's on the tip of my tongue to take shape. Those who have fallen asleep are at peace, those who can't sleep hang suspended on the night's echoes. A bolt of lightning strikes on the horizon, at the most inaccessible point in the sky. The clouds quiver. Several trees beyond the steps bow down before the wind. I suddenly feel cold. I stand up. Slowly I climb back down the worn-out steps. I'm in no hurry to get anywhere. The sea will always be waiting at the same spot, just beyond the steps. At the place where light and darkness join together. Instead of going along the sea, I head towards the jetty. I count my steps. Forty-one, forty-two, forty-three....I walk the entire length of the jetty's tiled walls. I arrive at the metal railings and stop. I place my hands on the railings. I examine the slender prow of the ferry on my right. Despite being tied to the jetty with thick ropes, it's rocking in the arms of the waves. Perhaps, like me, it too was unaware that the station had closed. It came here with its head full of dreams, spouting smoke, sounding its horn. It threw down its anchor. And never left again. But a boundless sea stretched before it. It could set sail. It could find itself new jetties (could it?). There is a loud crash of thunder from the direction of the Marmara Sea. Before its echo has subsided, another crash follows it. I want to know the meaning of thunder, like I want to know the meaning of everything. The meaning of the sea, the meaning of the dark, the meaning of letters and notes. The meaning of going, staying, forgetting, remembering. Only then could I approach the sea without fear. I could venture a little further, and stroll up and down the seafront where the young couple were just walking hand in hand, for as long as the waves' naked voice continues. The seafront looks as though it's inside the sea. The waves climb up it, then back away. The train station too becomes a part of the sea. A train station that has come from many layers below ground, from unknown times, from ten years, a hundred years, a thousand years in the past. It looks like a sunken ship, harboring hidden treasure behind its doors, and at the same time it's preparing to set sail at any moment, inflating its towers like sails. Wherever it's going, it can take me there too. And instead of waiting around for an uncertain future, Hayala, who's dreaming of traveling, can come with me. Does time flow the same for everyone, I don't know. One day I can discover that too. I take my phone out of my pocket. It's only then that I realize how cold my fingers are. With numb hands, I type in my pin. I find Hayala's number. The digits, which begin with zero, five, three, two, don't mean anything by themselves, but, when put together, they turn into something that means Hayala. That meaning latches onto the wind, flows over the Bosphorus like a light, and lands inside a telephone on the opposite shore. The telephone rings inside a bag. The bag vibrates on an armchair. The ringtone gets longer and louder. I remember similar scenes in films. I've seen it countless times, the phone ringing endlessly and, just when you're convinced that no one will pick up, a hand finally reaching out. A breathless voice comes from the other end. Boratin, she says, are you okay? I'm fine Hayala, I reply. Are you sure you're okay, is everything all right? she repeats. I'm fine, calm down, I say. I don't know, she says, you usually text me, when I saw your call at this time of night I thought something was up. Nothing's up. I crossed over from one side of Istanbul to the other. I was planning to get on a train and go somewhere far away for a while. The door of the train station closed in my face. I'm grounded here. Boratin, where are you? Where am I? They told me I was born from the sea, or at least, when I opened my eyes in the hospital, that's what I figured they were saying to me. I'm standing beside that sea. I'm at the train station, I say. Which train station? she says, I don't get it, which train station? Haydarpaşa Train Station, I reply. Hayala falls silent as she considers what to say. Of the scores of questions racing through her mind, she chooses the most innocuous. Is that what that howling in the background is, she says, the sound of the waves and the wind? Yes, I say, your voice sounds muffled too, as though you're somewhere far away instead of Istanbul. No Boratin, she says, I'm not far away, you know that. I know, I reply. I'm aware that our words have double meanings. I'm not far away either, I add. Shall I come and get you, she says. I can hear a song in the background. Someone is singing in a haunting voice. *Wake up, bare your face to the rain on the window / Let a cloudburst peel the toothmarks off your lips.* I can make out the tone of a Gibson guitar, I have one at home, but I don't recognize the singer's voice. Are you at the rehearsal, I say, or in a bar? The rehearsal's over, I'm back at home, says Hayala, what's up? Nothing, I say, when I heard music I thought you were out. Shall I turn it off? she asks. No, I say. I want to know who that singer with the faraway voice is. Hayala may be taking a sip of water, or she may be taking a drag of her cigarette. It's you Boratin, she says, I'm listening to your recordings. This is one of the songs I'm rehearsing for the concert this weekend. I remain silent. Hayala doesn't say anything either. We listen to the song together. *Wake up, bare your face to the rain on the window / If growin' used to it's another name for death / Don't let that same old violet in your hair fade and wear you down.* The music of the guitar and the piano interweave. Fingers sweep across the air. We contemplate the double meaning of the sounds. Meanings that we know exist but that we can't quite fit into. When the song is finished we return to our own words. Hayala, I say, it's cold here, the wind is howling. How long have you been there, she says. I don't know, I say, what time is it? It's past midnight, she replies. That late, I say. Boratin, says Hayala, she pauses for a moment before continuing, then adds, stay there, I'm coming to get you, okay? It's only then that I realize, Hayala's voice sounds like Bessie Smith's. It's husky, and deep. Come, I say, come and get me. Wait for me somewhere away from the wind, she says, I won't be long. She hangs up. I put my hands that have turned dry in the cold into my pockets. I stand on the station steps and gaze at the aged marble, the wooden doors, the large balconies. I can't see the station's towers anymore. Dark clouds descend and gradually enclose the entire building in their embrace. A drop falls onto my face. A raindrop.

# GLOSSARY

ABLA: An affectionate term of respect used for an older sister or older woman.

BEY: A formal term of respect used for a man, equivalent to Mr.

PIŞMANIYE: A kind of halva-like candy floss.

RAKI: Turkey's national drink, made of distilled aniseed.

SIMIT: Small loaf of ring-shaped bread, covered with sesame seeds. Extremely popular in Turkey.

# Timeline of Some Dates in *Labyrinth* and in Turkey

6000 BC  The earliest manufactured mirrors were made out of volcanic glass in Anatolia (modern-day Turkey).

3400 BC  The first known writing emerged in ancient Sumer, in Mesopotamia.

380 BC  The Greek philosopher Plato created the first alarm clock, which utilized water.

295 BC  The Library of Alexandria was founded. It is said to have been burned down many times over the ensuing centuries, first in 48 BC by the Roman

general Julius Caesar, then around 390 AD by Pope Theophilus of Alexandria, and then in 642 AD by the order of Caliph Omar.

33 AD     Crucifixion of Jesus in Golgotha.

41 AD     Death of the Virgin Mary.

324     The founding of the city of Constantinople (present-day Istanbul) by the Roman Emperor Constantine. It became the capital city of the Roman Empire.

1348     The construction of Galata Tower during an expansion of the Genoese colony in Constantinople.

1453     The Fall of Constantinople, the triumph of the Ottoman Empire, and the end of the Byzantine Empire.

1478     Topkapı Palace was opened as the Imperial Palace of Ottomans in Istanbul.

1499     Creation of the *Pietà*, the sculpture by Michelangelo, which depicts the body of Jesus on the lap of his mother, the Virgin Mary. The sculpture is housed in Vatican City within Rome.

1510     The first modern clock was invented by Peter Henlein in Nuremberg, Germany.

1549     Marguerite de Navarre, the princess of France and the Queen of Navarre, died at the age of fifty-six.

1876     Alexander Graham Bell, Scottish-born American scientist, invented the telephone.

| 1909 | The Haydarpaşa railway station was constructed by the sea on Istanbul's Asian side. Eight years later, the station was severely damaged in a fire. |
|------|---------------------------------------------|
| 1922 | The end of the Ottoman Empire. |
| 1923 | Foundation of the modern Turkish Republic by Atatürk. |
| 1926 | Mehmed VI Vahideddin, the last Ottoman sultan, died in exile in Sanremo, Italy. |
| 1934 | Women in Turkey gained full universal suffrage, earlier than in most other countries. |
| 1937 | Bessie Smith, American blues singer, died in a car accident in Mississippi at the age of forty-two. |
| 1955 | The worst pogrom against the non-Muslim (Greek, Armenian, Jewish) population in Istanbul lasted for two days. Dozens of people were murdered, dozens of women were raped, more than five thousand homes and businesses were destroyed. Most of the non-Muslim population in Istanbul had to leave Turkey. |
| 1960 | The Turkish army staged the first coup d'état against the authoritarian, antisecular, conservative government, which had been in power for ten years. The military, led by young army officers, executed three leading politicians, including the prime minister. |
| 1969 | American astronaut Neil Armstrong set foot on the Moon. |

1971    The Turkish army staged another coup d'état, with the aim of stopping a rising progressive movement that was very much influenced by the 1968 movements in Europe. After the coup, three leaders of a socialist youth movement were executed in what was seen as an act of revenge for the execution of three politicians in 1960. In a demonstration of the shift in the army's politics over the course of the decade, the leader of new conservative party supported the army's intervention and called the executions "three for three."

1973    Construction of the Bosphorus Bridge, in Istanbul, which connects Europe and Asia. To date, some five hundred people have committed suicide by jumping off from the 210-foot-high bridge into the sea.

1977    The May Day celebration of Workers' Day at Taksim Square in Istanbul was attacked by state-supported secret groups, and thirty-four people were murdered. Still, progressive movements in Turkey continued to proliferate.

1980    The Turkish army intervened in government with a third coup d'état, this one supported by NATO. On the morning of the coup, CIA Ankara station chief Paul Henze allegedly cabled Washington, saying, "our boys did it." The military regime executed fifty people, instituted widespread torture, and imprisoned some one million people. The aim was to quash free-minded social movements and initiatives in a country that was strategically important to the United States during the Cold War.

1984    The Kurdish civil war started. Fighting with the Turkish army has claimed forty thousand lives so far. The Kurdish population is nearly a quarter of the whole country, and their national identity, including their language, had been officially denied by the state. Public use of the Kurdish language continues to be restricted.

1988    The first gigantic shopping mall in Istanbul was opened. Currently there are 114 shopping malls in the city.

1993    The Madımak Hotel in the city of Sivas in central Turkey was attacked and set on fire by Islamist mobs. Thirty-seven intellectuals, artists, writers, and singers were killed. Some lawyers for the attackers would later join the Islamist government that is still in power.

1994    In Seattle, American singer Kurt Cobain died by suicide at the age of twenty-seven.

2000    It was revealed that a Sunni Hizbullah group in Istanbul kidnapped dozens of people, tortured them, and buried their bodies in the militants' family houses.

2001    Yavuz Çetin, a Turkish blues and psychedelic singer, ended his life by jumping off the Bosphorus Bridge at the age of thirty.

| 2002 | The Islamist Justice and Development Party (AKP) came to power in Turkey, and has been ruling the country ever since. Its leader, President Recep Tayyip Erdoğan, talks of reviving the Ottoman Empire's glory. Under his rule, Turkey has become the biggest jailer of journalists in the world. |
|---|---|
| 2010 | Haydarpaşa railway station caught fire and closed down. The government's intention to turn the station's stately building into a shopping mall or a fancy hotel caused protests. Haydarpaşa solidarity groups are watching the process. The World Monuments Fund, a New York–based heritage preservation organization, placed the railway terminal on its 2012 Watch list, drawing attention to the uncertain future of the historical site. |
| 2011 | The Syrian civil war broke out with the direct involvement of foreign countries. A coalition inlcuding the USA, UK, Turkey, Saudi Arabia, and Qatar aimed to overthrow the Assad regime but the violence only tore the country apart and fomented the rise of the radical movement ISIS. Currently there are four million Syrian immigrants in Turkey. |
| 2013 | The biggest revolt in Turkish history took place in Istanbul. It began as a protest to prevent Gezi Park in Taksim Square from being demolished and turned into a shopping mall. Then it turned into a common protest against the government's |

reactionary and authoritarian policies. During the two-week occupation of the park, revolt spread across the country, with the ultimate participation of four million people. Police killed eight young people, wounded four thousand others, and arrested another five thousand. In the end the government had to cancel its shopping mall project for the park.